# The Story of Ganador

# The Story of Ganador

## Part One of Trilogy

**This is the story of the life of a Spanish State Stallion. A story that proves 'fairy tales really can come true'.**

**Norma Grimes**

Published by Norma Grimes.

THE STORY OF GANADOR

ISBN 978-8-460-67789-5

Book formatted by www.bookformatting.co.uk.

# Contents

In memory of:

Nuno Oliveira

Fernando Sommer d'Andrade

Manuel Sabino Duarte

Antony Dent

# Acknowledgements

I would like to thank the following without whose help it would not have been possible to write this book.
Geoff, Samantha, the amazing horsemen of the Iberian Peninsula, the family of Ursula Bruns, Sue, Francisco Tineo Vasquez, Val Thornber, Lorraine Mace, Kit Rushton, Peter Brooks, S. Triggs, D Schwager, N. Jimenez and Veterinary Consultants Vetequin Estepona Spain.

Literature
The Spanish Horse Fernando D'Andrade
Xenophon… works of

Artwork by Sue Triggs

# About The Author

Norma is a professional musician and freelance writer on classical equitation. She lives in Andalucia with husband Geoff and daughter Samantha… where she keeps the love of her life Iberian Horses. She founded the Andalucian Stud UK and studied classical riding in Portugal and Vienna. Norma is an associate of the Royal College and a Licentiate of the Royal Academy and has taught in colleges within the UK.

# Prelude

*This is the story of the life of Ganador V, Spanish State stallion. Born in a century when nobility hath no purpose.*

I found Ganador in a Gypsies scrap yard, his stable a ramshackle cabin, his use a guard horse. Although chained to a wall - every breath he took and every movement he made displayed his great superiority. Despite his poor physical appearance it was plain to see that here was no ordinary earthly horse, here was a horse from another age, the age of chivalry and bravery. His ancestors once led armies into battle, were the chosen mounts of Kings, Commanders and Emperors. In the seventeenth and eighteenth centuries he was the most sought after fighting horse in Europe – his name, the Battle Horse of Kings. Ganador was the type of horse one is fortunate to meet once in a lifetime.

I hope everyone who reads this account of Ganador's life and times will remember his extraordinary magic forever... And this is his story, a story that proves 'fairy tales really can come true.'

'After God we owe our allegiance to the horses'
Hernandez Cortes. 16 C Spanish General

**Ganador and Norma, 1981. Horse of Kings and Emperors'.**
**Brave, fearless and incredibly noble.**
**The type of horse one is fortunate to meet once in a lifetime.**

# 1. 'Jerez'

*Jerez de la fronterra Andalucia Spain July 7 1973*

It was the last day of my holiday with Mum and Dad in that magical city of Jerez de la fronterra. To escape the afternoon sun we sat in a shaded Moroccan style café set amongst tall jacaranda trees. The café was set in the grounds of Parque Gonzalez Fontoria, close to the fairground and flamenco district. We sat outside, under the trees where we could see riders and carriages passing by.

Every one of the male riders looked stunningly handsome with refined facial features and an arrogant way of riding or turning the head. The men were exactly like their sleek horses; proud and superior. I could imagine them whispering…

'The past is not forgotten, in this distant corner of Europe, where tradition is kept alive'

"The men resemble peacocks" Mum said admiringly. I knew what she really meant… The male riders had an aura of nobility, they were proud, unmoving. Their rigid stance never wavered under the glaring light of the sun.

"Well heeled peacocks" said Dad with a smile. He was correct, for it would be impossible to take part in such colorful daily parades without owning fine horses, stables and land, perhaps even employing grooms too.

"Just look at the ladies! Whether in pretty dresses or riding costume the ladies of Jerez always look elegant" Mum adored this part of Andalucia, loved  everything it stood for, heartland of

3

flamenco… colorful fiestas… capital of the Andalucian horse.

"Jerez is Andalucia" she exclaimed "All rolled into one. Try to feel the simmering excitement… it's everywhere" she walked to the front of the paved area and said "Listen… to the sound of bells on the driving horses" she held up her finger the way she always did, and I listened. For a moment no-one moved. The air was alive with cheerful cadenzas from hundreds of tinkling bells and in the distance a Flamenco Guitarist strummed the opening chords of a Malaguena "Jerez has a magical charm, all of its own" Unfortunately Dad broke the spell as he always did, he wasn't a dreamer like Mum and me. Dad was ruled by time, by the clock. A practical, let's get on with it man forever planning the next move.

"How about staying right here for afternoon tea, and then strolling across the park to see the jousting tournament?"

"Sounds perfect" Mum smiled sitting back in her chair "The heat wears me out"

Dad looked to me now "Air conditioning and horses Norma. What do you think?"

"Sounds good"

"That's settled then"

In reality I wanted to return home, to my farm on the Yorkshire moors. How I longed to leave the heat and brightness of inland Spain. I wanted to gaze at the morning mists as they flooded into the valley, like ribbons of silver, wild and free, to smell the freshness of the moors… to hear the blackbirds sing… to be with Geoff and the horses.

"Only a few more hours to go; try and relax" Mum always said sensible things.

"But I can't relax before a flight" As I said these words, I didn't know my destiny would change forever because of that final afternoon.

At four o'clock we walked across the park, to enjoy the jousting - at least that's what I kept telling myself. I was feeling hot and tired, but I had to go through the motions of appearing to enjoy this last treat of Dad's. We arrived a few minutes late at the jousting hall, but once inside the foyer a handsome King came over to meet us. He thanked us for attending his games, and then went back to his throne where he drank a never ending supply of Jerez sherry. I'll never forget the crown he wore, it was cardboard and painted gold. His robes had seen better days too.

"You once had a crown like that" Mum whispered "I made it for the school nativity play" I had to bite my tongue so as not to laugh. But the King was very kind, and gave us special tickets for the front row. Holding our glasses of sherry tightly, we fumbled our way down the steps and sat waiting for the games to begin.

The lights gradually dimmed, the hall went black… any chatter died away. Then I heard a beautiful sound, a solo voice singing to the heavens, unaccompanied and incredibly moving.

"Such a pure voice" whispered Mum "Reminds me of Easter and the processions. It's always unforgettable to hear a Saeta" His cante pierced the silence… and for a few moments nothing mattered except the voice… the haunting melody. I wanted the voice to go on and on, but then the sounds of flamenco shattered the quiet with gay Sevillanas at the same time as spotlights over the arena grew brighter.

The solo voice had now become a guitarist. He created dazzling counter rhythms, amidst taps and claps of dancers. At that moment lights danced on the figures of a horse and rider that came galloping into the arena. They circled once then halted and bowed in front of the handsome King who sat at the head of a banqueting table. I can't remember any details about the rider - but I will never forget the horse. "Just look at his mane!" Mum sounded astonished "I never imagined such horses existed… not anymore"

His silken mane was heavy in gold braid, thick wild curls hanging almost to the ground. Even in the fierce heat of a Spanish Summer, he sent shivers running up and down my spine. Every line of his exquisite bone structure shouted of fine breeding. This was surely the same horse as painted by the great masters, whose exploits in combat had known no equal. His name: The Battle Horse of Kings… And he was awesome.

"Watch his movement, never mind his mane" interrupted Dad

"He soars through the air like a bird" I knew what he meant, his steps hovered, they were almost of the air and not the ground, as if at any moment he would spread his wings and fly.

When he galloped his whinnies thrilled me, for he sang from his heart, melodious, bell like cries.

"The flamenco group can't compete with this lad!" Dad smiled, he pointed to the artists who sat back in their chairs enjoying the spectacle before them. But I wasn't paying attention, not anymore. I closed my eyes and listened to the horse. His cries were nothing less than rapture, of pure joy. The horse was enjoying showing off his master.

"It's his Song of the Earth" I whispered "His melody is hauntingly beautiful. Nothing like a whinny" By this time I had fallen in love with this creature and I made a wish… that one day I would own such a horse.

I remember pretending to enjoy the games, unable to think of anything but the display horse. After the interval the horse entered once more, and again I never noticed his rider. For I gazed at a horse from another time, a time that began somewhere in mythology, a forgotten world steeped in legend and superstition. In a strange way he was frightening. It must have been his enormous eyes, supremely intelligent eyes, brilliant and staring.

"Look at his beautiful, black eyes" Mum seemed hypnotized by this strange horse "Watch how they consider every detail. He doesn't miss a thing"

I watched light dance and shimmer through his silken mane, casting a magical silver pool around him. When he collected himself together he looked as a cat preparing to jump, his movements were nothing like the forward going earth bound paces of present day horses. I thought of my own horses, at home in England, and wondered if they would even recognize such a creature as a fellow horse?

"Always thought the Baroque lines were dead as dinosaurs – But obviously not" Dad knew his horses, and I listened carefully "He could have stepped out of a fairy book, this is what the program says:"

Dad handed the program to me. At the bottom of the page were written the following words:

*"Bred for bravery and beauty, Baroque Cartuhano, Pure Spanish"*
*'It should be plainly seen, that the Spanish horse enjoys carrying its rider and being watched by spectators' 1677, a riding manual.*

As I read these words I knew I watched history repeating itself, right here before my eyes. Perhaps a few admirers of the old Spanish horse still possessed horses from ancient blood lines? Horses whose ancestors had led armies into battle or carried Kings, and I remember feeling a glow of excitement.

The moment the show ended, I returned to earth with a jolt, remembering I was flying home in less than twelve hours.

"There's plenty of time to drive Mum home, check on the time of your flight and then get to the airport" I could always depend on Dad, he planned everything, he always would... until... I stopped myself thinking this thought, he wasn't going anywhere yet, not for a long time. He worked in Spain for most of the year as a designer of precision tools for aircraft engines. I never fully understood what he did, because it didn't seem important, not then.

"What a splendid show" Mum smiled as she took my arm, she looked exhausted so delicate and vulnerable, yet really she was just the opposite. She was mentally strong; physically she looked of fragile appearance which always concerned me. But she had a habit of bouncing back, usually far quicker than I did. Nevertheless I still felt guilty for keeping her out shopping in the heat... and for going back home.

Why does saying goodbye to my parents never become any easier?

And why does returning back home make me feel guilty? I know its old fashioned but I think families should stay together. Maybe one day, I might return to Andalucia, or Mum and Dad will retire to the farm. Who knows? On the way to the airport Dad told

me of the growing unrest in Portugal "If you travel there love…
You should be careful"

"What do you mean Dad, careful?"

"It isn't wise to be seen with anyone labeled fascist, and that
includes people owning land or large properties. I know you have
friends there with horses who might own land. Unless people fall
into the category of poor and uneducated, they may be watched,
especially round Lisbon"

"But why will they be watched?"

"Leaders of the Communist party are returning to Portugal -
from exile"

"Where's exile?"

"I think Franco's days are numbered, there could be thousands
of his followers getting out of Spain by way of Extremadura.
Portugal might become a meeting place"

"I wonder what they're planning"

"Their chief objective must be to escape trial, their second
intention is probably power, sufficient power to form a coalition
movement with the Portuguese armed forces which could lead to a
nasty purge on the wealthy. My advice is to keep your head down
and remember the police will be with the workers. It's just a
warning"

"No-one's said anything Dad"

"Just remember that sensible people don't draw attention to
themselves"

"But Portugal always seems so laid - back"

"Portugal is a relaxed country, but do take care. This is their
way, it's how they take power, calculated unhurried"

But I quickly forgot Dads words whenever I thought of the
display horse, the horse that had molded the course of civilization
with his bravery and his nobility. Somehow he made everything
else seem unimportant.

"I really enjoyed the show Dad"

"Spain knows how to put a show on, I'll agree with that"

Following that day memories of the horse refused to go away,
and images of him just kept on returning; he became my fantasy, an

echo from the past, a kind of fountain within my imagination. I had to learn more about the battle horse of Kings, I could not be alone in my wish to find other horses like him. Surely there just had to be someone who held the key to his history and whereabouts?

# 2 Antony

*February 24th. 1974. Yorkshire Moors.*

Six months after my holiday, something definite is at last starting to happen I think I may have found someone who feels exactly as I do. His name is Antony and his age, seventy five! He sounds so full of life that it's difficult to imagine he is so very old. His letters are really helpful and informative. Antony tells me he enjoyed my article on 'Riding without Reins' and to keep on writing. He also tells me to contact him if I need help when researching. How kind!

Antony lives in France and writes on ancient history and horse breeding. His pet subject is equestrian combat and he wants to come to Yorkshire to spend a few days with me - "To find out what you are all about!" At last the wonderful process of understanding the breed is starting to unfold.

*March 27. 1974.*

It was a freezing cold day in late March when I first met Antony. I'll never forget his dramatic arrival. His taxi crawled into the stable yard at nothing more than a snails pace, through a thick milky mist. Neither will I forget the red faced driver who said he should charge double for driving to the top of a mountain.

"I never drive higher than the steeps, and I won't be coming back." The driver shouted angrily.

"Some people are so rude" I tried to apologize, whilst directing looks of hatred towards the driver and helping Antony out of the taxi.

"Avoid loud and aggressive people dear" Antony looked away from the driver. He acted as if the red faced man wasn't there. "Vexations to the spirit" He slipped the taxi fare onto the back seat, retrieved his case from the boot and gave me a big hug.

"It's a beautiful world out there" he called out to the departing driver "Enjoy your day, I know I will!"

After unpacking I made him a pot of tea and we sat in the lounge and talked, or Antony talked. He told me about his books and his passions which were horse breeding and the history of the Spanish horse.

"Better hobby than stamp collecting" he said taking a long breath "And I can earn a few pence with my books - always supposing the proof editor is decent. You see I tend to write in German and sometimes they do a terrible job, you wouldn't believe it." He said grimacing "But first we talk of horses, far more interesting than proof editors"

"According to Daphne, and she knows 'everything,' the Iberian horse reached perfection as a battle horse before the XV C." he said sipping his third cup of tea. "It was this noble animal which was taken to Italy by the Spaniards for their wars in the kingdom of Naples and with which they defeated the French cavalry. Everyone wanted him, and no price was too high to pay. His fame was such that he became the most sought after horse in Europe, and thought of as the only proper mount for Kings or noblemen. Like vintage champagne he was!" he said laughing.

"Horses taken to the New World will have been of Spanish descent, which subsequently evolved in the Mustang and most other American breeds. A strong sound horse he must have been, with good dense bone and rock hard feet. The old Spanish horse was wanted by every country in Europe as a means of improving different breeds, which he made a damn good job of. The most important European breeds can be traced back to the Iberian peninsular. Without a doubt they were thought of as the best horses in the World. The result of all this buying was vastly decreased numbers and blood lines of perhaps a lesser standard. They were so appreciated by foreigners that exportation had to be banned and all mares had one ear clipped to make them easily recognizable"

"His downfall was in part due to his outstanding success, that and breeders greed. Can't blame them for not refusing to get rich, can you? Unfortunately breeders found themselves without the established proven blood lines, and had to turn to horses not up to the standard required."

Antony paused, before changing the subject from horses to editors, with a few of his latest horror stories thrown in "Unbelievable they are. Be very careful when you want to publish dear" he shook his fist and flushed a very unhealthy red. "Get rich quick guys most of them, exactly the same as the breeders were! But now I'm interrupting my story." Antony took a sip of tea and breathed deeply before going on "Returning to the horses, further weakening of the old blood lines continued as warriors started wearing armor and carrying heavy weapons. Considering the average knight in armor weighed in at thereabouts twenty five stone plus, the most important item on the agenda; or in a horse, began to be weight carrying ability, and this is where the cob came in. You see men in armor found mounting damn difficult; and the smaller cob type fitted the bill perfectly. Last thing they wanted was a spirited horse that pranced around... as you can well imagine. Difficult job it must have been to mount, what do you think?" I knew it really didn't matter what I thought and poured him yet another cup of tea.

"How kind my dear, I'm not boring you am I?"

"Oh no...What you are telling me is fascinating, please don't stop" By now I was taking notes of his every word.

"Intelligence and bravery were no longer needed, neither was agility. The battlefield changed, began to have different fighting methods. Sometimes fifty or more men and horses would be placed side by side in long straight lines, and then ordered to charge into enemy lines, it consisted of a front line, second line, so on. The military called this slaughter the 'equine tank,' but really the first line or two were on a suicide mission. But time waits for no man, or horse come to that" he took a deep breath before going on.

"All through history the horse has been a product of mans

meddling or adaptation; everything to suit mans needs. Not for the better either! Horses are expected to produce the greatest efforts, no matter what their history of conformation or soundness may be poor creatures. In central Europe along with the beginnings of fire power, horses were expected to pull tanks about. If the men couldn't shift the weight, the horses could… Which in turn led to a necessity for heavier horses with straighter hind legs; more pulling power you see. But yet another weakness was introduced, one more fault in conformation" for a few seconds Antony was silent.

"What a delicious aroma coming from the kitchen" he said "Is dinner early or late?"

"Is nine too late? I can make you a sandwich now" Antony looked tired following his marathon journey from France to Yorkshires moors all within twenty four hours.

"Not at all dear, gives me a chance to stretch my legs, and have a little snooze" he said as he walked to the staircase. Over dinner Antony steered the conversation in the direction of the health service, French style and the soaring costs of living. "If I had only known, I would have planned towards retirement much earlier. But sadly the gift of experience is only given to a man when his hair is grey" he said with a sigh "but the unexpected always happens and there is nothing surer than that."

After lunch the following day we resumed our chat, "The old type of Spanish horse is still around… if in the background" he said "Such horses can be seen pulling carriages at horse ferias. I presume they are owned by sherry barons, or the Spanish gentry. It was probably one of these animals you saw in Jerez, take your breath away they do! That so many blood lines – or so few, depending on how you look at it – have survived, is mainly due to a few breeders in religious orders, principally the Carthusian monks of Jerez.

Only the Carthusian monks had the patience, determination, knowledge - call it wisdom if you like to maintain the traditional qualities of the breed. And they refused all experimentations in cross breeding!

Spanish studs were severely in decline by the nineteenth century... cross breeding had become common, usually with Danish or German horses! Good for military parades... or so they thought! You see the noble Spanish horse was no longer bred for his expertise in battle. He'd become a horse for pleasure, bred only for his beauty. But by then it was too late, the studs had lost their pure bred's. Thank goodness the Carthusian monks were determined to breed only from the old lines. But in the mid 1970... the monks left Jerez. And their precious stock of pure Spanish lines went to three breeders - which I know of, Dr Ruy Andrade of Portugal, Salvatierres, and the Terry stud of Spain.

Within Portugal, the story is slightly different. Due to the bullfight on horseback, the earlier selection was carried on and this saved the original type of battle horse. The Lusitano as he's called is still selected for the exercises needed in combat and not for his beauty"

"So the selection was different in Portugal?"

"I'm sure it was... Until the civil war"

"What happened then?"

"Many of the best lines were lost... to the meat markets"

"The Horse of Kings has had a tragic history. Just imagine, he fought mans battles for thousands of years and now there's no place for him. But there are a few breeders who still try to replicate the qualities of the earlier 'genet' horse. Andrade bred horses can still be seen, fighting in the bullrings of Portugal. You see, he is the perfect horse on which to fight, frightened of nothing and keeps the rider away from the bull. A trained fighting horse is worth an incredible sum of money, supposing you can find one that is! Today he is often crossed with the Arab, for greater speed to match the faster bulls!    Although.... the present day Masters within Portugal still train their Iberian stallions in the old combat style. Give thrilling displays of high school work, exciting to behold. But I know he's still around, if in small numbers." Anthony sipped his coffee and tasted one of my scones. "Delicious" he said "I adore homemade scones." After his snack Antony quickly led the conversation back to horses.

"Today, mans needs are for longer striding, more tranquil horses. You see modern man rides for pleasure or competition. The elevated paces and fiery tempers of the Baroque Iberian horse are not always suited to present day competition, or to present day riders come to that! But there are, even today, a few private breeders who try to reproduce these unique characteristics by using the closest blood lines to the horses that carried Kings"

In the afternoon of the third day, I drove Anthony to the nearest station, his stay had ended much too quickly and I felt sad to see him depart. He suddenly looked so very frail and vulnerable in the grey light of a winter's day.

"Don't worry about me" he said as though reading my thoughts "I've had a splendid time. Now I'm off to look for a piece of land in Cleveland, my son lives there. It's for when I return home" he said with a happy grin "Fed up with France" he shook his head and grimaced.

"Do remember I'm at your service should you need any help or research with that writing your planning" he placed a brown paper parcel in my hands "a little something for your kindness dear" he said putting his hand on my arm. "And don't forget Daphne, encyclopedia she is, does all my research, as well as writing her own stuff. We writers keep together because we damn well have to." He said before boarding the train.

My last sight of Antony was of him lighting his pipe in a non smoking compartment, oblivious to everything but his newspaper. As the train pulled away I didn't let a moment of time slip by before opening the brown paper parcel Antony had given me. He had carefully packed three out of print books two were about history and the third the Iberian horse. The author of the top book was Daphne, and it was written in German. I made my way to the car park, sat turning pages for a while and watched the train disappear into the distance. I would miss Anthony.

My only comfort was that I now had an idea of where the remaining battle horses may be. And so I carried on searching, reading every scrap of information that came my way. As the years passed by the mental picture of my fantasy horse, remained exactly the same, 'he' never faded away. In his last letter Antony told me to 'keep on probing, you find these horses in the strangest of places' He also gave me five key names to look out for in their breeding, and pointed out that the 'mares blood lines are much more important than the stallions. Do keep searching dear, you'll find him in the end!'

*'He trots the air the earth sings when he touches it'*
*William Shakespeare.*

# 3. The Advert

*Toby Jug Farm Yorkshire Moors. March 13 1980*

It was a freezing cold day in early March, the kind of day when the view from my moorland farm could only be described as magical… some would say surreal. Frost covered the surrounding moors and ribbons of chiffon mist shrouded the lower valley.

"It must be time to put the coffee on, or so my freezing hands tell me"

"Good idea Norma, I've only to fill water buckets…"

Leaving Sue to finish morning stables, I returned to the house, picked up the post from behind the door, and tore the plastic cover from around Horse and Hound, my weekly must read. The magazine fell open, and there before my eyes were the words I had waited to see… For so long.

*Ganador V. State Registered Spanish Stallion, Finest Baroque blood lines… Hosco-Nevada. Tel….*

When I read the advert, I felt as though the earth had stopped spinning. Can this be happening after almost seven years? I studied the words once more just to make sure it was there, reading each word very slowly, over and over again. It really was there definitely not imagination…

"The water pipes frozen" called Sue from the stable yard "I'll have to fill buckets from the kitchen." Sue always brought me down to earth, especially in the mornings.

"Can you take over Sue?" I replied "Just do what has to be done.

I have to make a phone call. Please Sue?" Then I turned away, with one thought on my mind… The mysterious Ganador. Before walking over to the phone I scribbled down a few opening questions, such as price, age and past owners. As I started to dial the number, my hands began to tremble uncontrollably, 'try to remain calm' I told myself 'breathe deeply, this could be the chance you've been waiting for.

After what seemed to be forever, but was only the fourth ring, the breathless voice of a man answered.

"Scrap yard!" the man said in a matter of fact way.

"But I'm ringing about a horse – not scrap" Already I could feel my heart thumping rapidly.

"Tis about Ganador?" he said with a sudden laugh.

"Yes it is" I found myself struggling with the words I wanted to say "I've just read the advert."

"Good Oss he is; never had a better one. He's a real class stallion, to be sure." He spoke defiantly, as though warning me to be careful of what I asked. "To be sold at a reasonable price, due to circumstances beyond our control" he swiftly added. His voice had a peculiar sing song dialect, a set rhythm. I'd heard the same strange accent before.

"Where are you?" I asked him, my carefully planned questions seemed to vanish from my mind. "We will be driving from Yorkshire."

"Yorkshire!" he repeated, his guard slipping "You've got a long drive ahead. Well over three hundred miles south we are lady. If you want to know any more about Ganador ring later, Dads about after four. Morning to you" he said before terminating my call.

I stood against the phone for a minute trying to place his accent. Then I remembered as if it were yesterday. It was the same sing song twang I'd heard at Appleby horse fair, the rhyming slang of travelling men, arguing long and heatedly concerning the price of a horse. I remembered listening to the men, fascinated by their rhyming speech and arrogant pride. I will never forget that day – Geoff had said "Fancy a drive up to Appleby fair?"

"Yes please" I said. So we drove up to Cumbria, the day was

Saturday and the fair already in full swing. It had started two days earlier, on the first Thursday after the first Tuesday in June. Geoff parked on Gallows hill, just outside the town where the fair spills out onto surrounding meadows. We walked in the direction of 'sellers run,' a roped off area where horses were trotted out, bought or sold. I wanted to stay and listen to the sales patter of the Gypsy men.

"Do we have to stand here?" Geoff looked fed up already "You know I hate crowds"

"Just a little longer… Please"

"Watch your bag, hold it to the front" he warned.

At that instant a travelling man pushed past me, he walked with a limp. I watched him step up onto a box to start off the next sale. He held up his hand and the crowd was suddenly still, I could tell he was admired by the way people around him hung onto his every word. And then I saw the horse, although I could only see him from a distance I knew he was very handsome – I also knew his color was silver grey. A boy led the horse; thick black curls cascading past his shoulders, a blood red scarf tied loosely around his neck.

There was something different about the boy. He had a very special gift, the gift of feel. His easy way of handling the fiery horse put the other men to shame. He and the stallion were as one whatever the horse did the boy would be at his side, whispering, cajoling but always fearless and always his friend. The frightened horse trusted the boy, and the boy loved the horse. Between the two I felt a special attachment. A joining together that helped him understand the behavior of the stallion far better than he understood the ways of the men around him.

"He must be a stallion Geoff, listen to his calls" His whinnies were sweet and melodious, first high then low and gentle. When the crowd saw the horse some of the men crawled under the barrier cheering and clapping, prodding his ribs, feeling his legs, looking to find blemishes.

"Anyone touching this oss does so at their own peril"

When they heard this warning the crowd stood back, and the

group of men inside the run scrambled to safety under the rope barrier.

"There's a red ribbon in his tail" whispered Geoff "I suppose it's one way to move a crowd"

Just at that moment a rough looking dealer stepped forwards "Where's the oss come from? He's not your type man" I could see he was a dealer by the way he looked at the horse – he never looked into his eyes.

"A Spanish King" the Gypsy replied "Look at his finely boned head, feel his silken mane. There has never been such a magnificent creature, never" Just as he shouted 'never' the horse exploded, first he plunged forwards then he reared up high, almost vertically, as though he might fall over backwards. And the crowd backed away from the horse, only the boy stayed by his side.

I watched the dealer pull the sellers sleeve twice, the signal to start bartering "Do you want to sell or do you not?" he said angrily. Instantly the crowd became silent they all wanted to hear his reply.

"How much money's in your pocket man?" The seller spoke to the crowd not the dealer. How they loved his mocking style "Or did I forget to mention his price?"

"You did, you did" the crowd jeered at the dealer whose face flushed purple.

"Show me the colour of your money - put your riches on this wooden box... We might start trading if we start at five thousand" And the dealer turned on his heel and walked away. Immediately the dealer disappeared amongst the crowd a tall elegant man bent under the rope and shook the Gypsies hand, he must have been waiting his chance.

"Unbelievable... He's got another buyer!" said Geoff, this time he pulled me closer to the man on the box.

"Now he's a well bred horse" The elegant man ran his fingers down the stallion's legs, looked at his teeth and touched his glossy mane "Like a fall of silk" he said, and the Gypsy eyed the man from his well shod feet to his classy fitted shirt.

"You are the kind of man I like to do business with" said the smiling Gypsy. I can see his thoughts; his twinkling eyes say it all.

He's imagining stacks of money. This man is wealthy, maybe filthy rich "You have money to spend Sir, can see fine breeding and only want the best. Am I right?" asked the Gypsy.

"I am looking to buy beauty. Class horses for use in films" The man steps closer to the horse, he reaches out to the stallion's neck offering friendship and the horse stands quietly now, it can feel no threat from this man "He could carry a King…"

"But could a King ride him?" muttered Geoff, he took hold of my arm and walked me away "Can we go now, as far away from this mob as possible?"

So we drove down Gallows hill into the road where the river runs through the town, it felt so peaceful after the fair. We sat on the river bank under some overhanging trees watching a never ending parade of colored horses coming down to its banks for washing. But my day was spoiled when a gang of youths arrived who just wanted to have fun. I saw one foal separated from its mother and manhandled into the fast flowing water…

"I wish we'd driven home. I'll never sleep tonight"

"Don't suppose they can all be rough louts – just most of them" Geoff sounded appalled………

"Norma!" Sues voice broke my thoughts, so I allowed the dream to slip away "Ready for elevenses?" She carried on spooning coffee into the mugs "You look worried" she said pointedly.

"I am." I sighed, and then I told her about the advertisement "Antony's been looking for years without success. The few Baroque lines that remain are out of his price range, even the veterinary officer in Jerez told him he was wasting his time… 'Pure Spanish lines have more or less vanished' the expert said 'There may be a few remaining in private stables but the old lines ancient history now. Gone but not forgotten as you say'

"So it is a fairy story – and it could be a dodgy one. Might it be possible to find the person who imported this Ganador?" Sue suggested helpfully. "Why not check out the Andalucian breed society, or the importers? Driving six hundred miles in a horsebox is a long way to go see a donkey in a shed!" and I had to agree. Sue had a gift for problem solving, sorting black from white as she liked to put it "How badly do you want to see this stallion?"

"Very badly" I replied "I've been dreaming of him for seven long years"

"Then grab your dream by the bollocks girl" Sue advised "Stop acting like a hermit and follow your dream, you've waited far too long." And so I did just that I went for it and followed my dream, I was on track once more.

After what seemed like several hours with the telephone pressed to my ear, I discovered the importer of Ganador who kindly passed on the precious telephone number of his first English owner. This came as a surprise, for his owner had a title: Sir Roland MacFee, famous in the racing world as a trainer. Shortly after midday, I stamped on my nerves breathed in deeply and dialed the number. A woman called Gloria picked up the phone; she sounded very kind "He's in the garden" she said "Can you wait one minute?"

"I'm ringing about a horse he used to own"

"He loves talking about horses. Who shall I say is calling?"

Following the formalities of introduction I plunged in with question one.

"I believe you imported a Spanish stallion name of Ganador?" But what if he claimed Ganador had been stolen from his yard... he seemed a very unlikely person to have sold a horse to a Gypsy.

"That is correct" he replied "And why do you ask - are you a writer?"

"I am in a way, although...." But I was too slow, this man loved to talk.

"I believe I'm the first Englishman since Charles the second to import two pure bred Andalucian's with Baroque family lines- I bought the pair some years ago from the most famous Yeguada in Spain. The pair had recently won a driving championship in Seville. So I paid a considerable sum of money, far too much!" he said "Lost my head I did... I was touring Spain with Gloria my wife looking for two good Andalucian horses to buy and bring back to England, when I came across this unbelievably beautiful Yeguada, a real eye opener it was. The horses were incredible, all prize winners and with perfect breeding. Used for driving they were. The head groom would take Gloria and me driving in the parks of Seville whenever we wished, and the pair of horses pulling our carriage were Ganador, aged three and his brother Papillon who was five – Do tell me if I'm boring you?"

"Oh no, this is interesting... Please carry on"

"There's one night I will never forget, the proprietor better known as the master invited the wife and I for a drive into Seville by moonlight... It was very late at night when spring was in the air and the scent of oranges was everywhere. Ganador and Papillon were put to the light carriage for the drive into Seville. The carriage and pair were a splendid sight, the horses wore garlands of flowers and the finest harness money can buy. Gloria said she had never seen such riches. I'll always remember that night, the sound of the pair trotting along the road, the relaxing sway of the carriage; moonlight shimmering on the river... It was so exciting. After we passed the Alcazar, the carriage paid a visit to the Patio De Los Naranjos, where the coachman told us a little of its history. 'In Moorish times' he said 'worshippers washed their hands and feet in the fountain under the orange trees before praying,' that coachman brought everywhere alive, such a fascinating person. Afterwards we made our way into the old town, weaving in and out through a maze of narrow white Calles. When the horses finally halted, the time was two a.m. and the sounds of flamenco were all around us. May as well admit it, I had never heard such emotional music before that night. Gloria said she felt possessed by its strange haunting sound"

"It's good to have memories" I said.

"I can still hear the carriage rattling, and the ringing sounds of horse shoes on cobbles. Even now I dream of that night."

"You make the drive sound... delightful, I can picture it all"

"A pleasant memory" he replied thoughtfully "Of a wonderful night... However, to return to the story, we adored Ganador right from the moment we set eyes on him, a real character always up to something. Majestic he was with a strange tendency to look you straight in the eyes as though he knew what you were thinking! His brother is the opposite, very quiet. Like chalk and cheese they are.

But it wasn't all 'delightful' as you put it – one of the saddest day's I can remember happened there amidst all that beauty and privilege. I don't know if it still goes on, but I hope not."

"Did something terrible happen?" I knew it had, his voice trembled and his words were full of emotion – something dreadful had taken place.

"The sounds and pictures of that day will be with me for the rest of my days. We were invited to watch the grading of young stock, there were ten. The officials sat round a table at the far end of the paddock. There were four of them, and I was told they came from Jerez. Each young horse was carefully measured, fetlock to knee, knee to elbow, elbow to shoulder – even the distance between their eyes! The eyes were considered very important. Then they marked the movements, grooms had to trot each young horse away and then towards the judges and so on. The measurements and paces were given a mark out of ten – nine exceptional, eight very good, seven above average. If the total marks came to seventy or more the horse was entered on the list of State Registered stallions."

"What if the marks came to below seventy...?"

"Two of the youngsters failed to reach the required standard" he paused as if reliving the scene. The eight that passed were led away to the blacksmiths yard. It was then I heard the mares, the mothers of the two that failed, they were pleading for their offspring– I never knew a horse could make such a sorrowful sound, human it was.

The grooms dug a deep grave filling it with lime, and those two young horses were shot, right there, under the old oak tree. Gloria almost collapsed – but the staff thought nothing of it. The stud manager told us the grading happened every year.

'The master cannot give his brand to second class animals' he said 'It is for the good of the Yeguada'

"Probably to do with the price" I said "No brand, means no registration papers, and a much lower price"

"I think you're right - It keeps the value artificially high. As if this was not enough I was taken up to the blacksmith's yard to witness the branding. Gloria said a firm 'No' but I stupidly went along. The whole thing was horrific… The grooms dragged each youngster in turn over to the forge, roped its legs and then dropped the poor thing to the ground. To prevent any movement they pulled the ropes tight and held the red hot branding iron down on its left thigh. Terrible it was, watching smoke rise and hearing their cries. I heard their skin crackling before it branded the mark of the master. The smell of burning flesh is shocking, unimaginable"

Sir Roland did not appear to be holding back on the topic of Ganador. It was time for the big question. "Can you tell me as to why you sold him and who owns him now?" There was a short silence, then, he said "So, Ganador is to be sold?" What could I say but "Yes" Then he said slowly "So you want to buy him?" "Perhaps" I ventured, thinking this is not going smoothly. He then asked me what I knew about the history of the breed and had I any experience with stallions. I told him I had fallen head over heels in love with the breed almost twenty years ago and of our yard on the Yorkshire Moors.

Sir Roland answered, but without enthusiasm. "I never wanted to sell the stallion, but Ganador suffered a series of accidents the last one being a back and stifle sprain. He ran into the rails of the stallion paddock; demolished a section he did, crashed through them like they were firewood. The rails were five feet high and damn strong. He must have become in a panic over something, had a temperament like fire!" he said reliving the past "Following his wild times he would suddenly became like an angel, if you know what I mean."

I must be crazy I thought, stark raving bonkers. No sane person would continue with this conversation. But I did, already I'd become fascinated by Ganador, by his past, his charisma. Already I knew I had to see him, despite everything his owner said. My only problem might be Geoff… but persuading Geoff would not be too difficult because Geoff possessed a weakness concerning fine - looking horses. He melted when beauty and spirit came together in a horse.

"Did he ever recover from his injuries?" I asked.

"After the last accident I had to keep him on box rest for many a month. Had a large loose box built for him with an external yard he could walk into. I thought it might encourage him to rest and stop him kicking the door. Ganador was not the type of horse who could stand behind a door for long. Always wanted to see what was happening!" he laughed. "It was then a travelling man started coming to the yard, came almost daily, 'Can I see Ganador - The Spanish Oss?' he always asked, said his name was Adams. The grooms told me he was a Gypsy and to be careful. After some weeks, he began to make bids for the horse, drove me mad he did. At the time I'd no reason to want to sell him, we all liked Ganador, far more intelligent than some people. He really was."

"When did you sell him?" I prompted. Not one to rush with replies, his past owner hesitated before replying.

"I can't answer that question because it wasn't like that. But let me tell you the rest of the story. When he recovered, he was walked then lunged for six weeks. After building up some muscle tone we introduced him to the saddle once more, walking up to the house and then back to the stables, on a loose rein with a carrot from the gardener - you know the kind of thing. But he began to rear on mounting," he spoke without enthusiasm and I heard a note of melancholy in his voice. "Unfortunately Ganador had other ideas about walking to the house."

"So he recovered?" I said, thinking it was all making sense, like a jigsaw puzzle when finally the pieces fit together "When did he go to his present home?" I asked, thinking what a fool I must be having this chat... With a man I didn't know... About a wild stallion I'd never seen.

Sir Roland interrupted my thoughts, he sounded angry "I suppose that darned man Adam's just waited for something to happen. He became very persistent with his bidding...I thought of getting the police in, but the grooms said it wasn't a good idea. His words were always the same 'There's always another day' he would say 'You may think different tomorrow!'

"One day my wife was riding Ganador up to the house, when he reared, stood straight up pawing the air... almost went over backwards. The wife had a nasty fall. She fell onto the stone cobbles…hasn't ridden since. So I began to listen to Adams. He told me he wanted to drive Ganador. I thought I saw a way out for the horse if he was only to be driven, so you see in the end Adams got what he wanted. We loved the horse but he never settled in here" Sir Roland said softly. I think I knew then that Sir Roland had allowed the man Adams to dominate him but now resented what he had done. What a colorful and sad past.

Spirited horses always come down the ladder, lower and lower with the quality of their owners. Men do not appreciate being made a spectacle of by any horse, thus it is better for a horse to act in a subdued manner, show good manners and let that certain something, called ' the spark of life' be gone. Sad but true. The horse is only used for sport today; dressage, show jumping, hacking quietly out. Rider's no longer want fierce horses that would be willing to lay down their lives for them, neither do they desire the qualities they once had, of courage and spirit. In today's world possessing either gives a horse a bad name most usually with the prefix 'crazy.'

Sir Roland took me by surprise when he said "I never gave Adams his State Registered Papers you know, did not want him using Ganador as a stallion" then he went on to say "If you like the looks of the stallion and buy him, I will post you his registration papers together with some photos of him in Spain. You know, I would much prefer someone like yourself to have Ganador, someone who loves the breed"

After thanking Sir Roland and promising I would be in touch 'if' we bought the stallion I replaced the receiver and retreated to the kitchen. Three cups of coffee later I rang Geoff with information about Ganador and Adams phone number, begging him to find where the yard was located.

"Horses don't live in scrap yards" Geoff said irritably.

"This one does. When you ring you will find out"

"Well I'm not driving the horsebox to the other end of England without proof"

"I have proof, his last owner told me the horse is with Gypsies"

"Gypsies, scrap yards and Spanish stallions make an unlikely trio… but I promise to ring" I breathed a long sigh of happiness. So it is true, it is possible for dreams to become reality.

"Remember what Antony said?"

"What did Antony say?"

"You find these horses in the strangest of places"

*'Wild Horses of Fire, what wings raised thee to the second power?'*

# 4. The Scrap Yard

*7 p.m. March 13 1980*

*"When carefully chosen, there is no horse in the world to match the Spanish horse. It is well formed from its pointed ears down to its hooves. One could not find a nobler animal. It has great strength, great courage, learns quickly, is agile, trots gracefully and has a prancing gallop. It is also nobler, and more affectionate. The Spanish horse is a horse fit for a King, whether to ride in ceremonial parade or to head his troops into battle. Duke Leopald has one of these horses, whose value is said to be the equivalent of a yearly income of a thousand tailors."*
*Duke of Newcastle 18C*

How the pendulum swings, when at one time every horse connoisseur in Europe would have given 'the yearly income of a thousand tailors' to purchase a well bred Spanish stallion. 'A horse fit for a King'. But times change and needs differ. Any 'carefully chosen' horse in today's world must first possess a sensible temperament, have ground covering paces, and more than average ability in the winning of rosettes. The name of the game in this modern world is called rosette hunting, certainly not leading troops into battle. Nobility, great courage, and prancing gallops are not at the top of any modern rider's equine shopping list – except for my own...

Shortly before eight o'clock that Friday evening, Geoff drove the horsebox onto the moorland road. There was a low rippling mist hovering above the roads surface. Freezing fog in March equaled dangerous driving conditions, but what could I expect when living at a height of twelve hundred feet? Geoff frequently said we lived in the clouds. Once we entered the mist there were no land marks, any details were hidden except for a few meters of road. The rules for staying alive were simple, dip headlights, lower gear, and proceed slowly, very slowly.

Suddenly and at a bewildering speed, a loud blast of engine noise flashed past, it sounded like an angry explosion in the empty silence of the moors. Geoff screamed to a stop, his eyes dazzled by the oncoming lights.

"Imbecile, didn't even lower his headlights" Geoff remarked angrily "Speeding townies on suicide missions" Geoff was correct, townies out for a run were the nightmare of local drivers, not a week went by without a mishap. The last accident had been fatal, a decapitation of a hells angel only nineteen years of age and testing his new bike over the moors.

"This road gives me the creeps; it's unlit, too narrow and has no grip. Hope this isn't one of your wild goose chases Norma?" muttered Geoff, already eating his second sandwich. There were many suitable replies I could have made, but I chose to remain silent "Ten more hours to drive then"

At the edge of the moor the country road dipped into a small village where story book cottages stood side by side with brightly lit roadside Inns. Following the village were the farms, large farms which served the town. All had fields with green identical grass, kept alive by constant spraying there was no place for delicate wild flowers or sweet smelling clover in the lowlands.

After descending into the lowest part of the valley, the icy cold turned to cloud and thin rain. The silence of the moors had gone... In its place I heard the noisy roar of the road and bewildering hum of life. Geoff said the new sounds were of people living normal lives, he said no-one lived on the moors, not by choice. Driving further south we passed trees and forests then pretty villages, that other world where sensible people lived in comfortable houses "No sensible person would live on top of the moors in a row of cottages filled with horses. People like comfort" So I handed him a third sandwich and put the radio on.

Shortly before midnight we headed due south on the motorway, and cruised gently along for a time. The never ending lights of the motorway quickly turned night into day, removing any tiredness I may have been feeling. After six hours driving, Geoff drew off the motorway and pulled into a lay-by. Wrapping horse blankets around our rapidly chilling bodies we made several, unsuccessful attempts to sleep. But sleep proved impossible, a damp penetrating cold made sure of that. Instead we drank coffee, ate all the sandwiches, and slowly became a little warmer.

What have I done, I thought, expecting Geoff to drive hundreds of miles in freezing cold temperatures to see a horse with a history of physical unsoundness, or even worse some mental instability?

As dawn began to break we were off again. Now only a few hours were left until we saw Ganador V in the flesh.

*

*March 14 South East England.*

"This is it!" Geoff said suddenly "The White Horse Inn, look out for an unmade track on the right with a scrap yard sign, it's painted white and fastened to a tree"

"Here it is" I felt shocked we were there. Geoff turned down a pathway just wide enough for the horsebox, where the sign 'Scrap Yard' hung from a dead tree - it was like visiting another world, a sad world. The landscape suddenly became a gloomy sight, depressing when compared to our hill farm where everything looked fresh and untouched with nothing and nobody except the hills and the moor.

Geoff parked the horsebox outside the scrap yard gate as instructed by Adams. It looked to be a busy industrial yard, with three caravans parked on the same area. The caravans were surrounded by mountains of humanities rubbish. On the left were

31

broken up cars and scrap metal, on the right a forest of skips filled with paper waste, squashed down with wet soggy mattresses.

"I think I must be mad" said Geoff despondently draining the last drops of coffee from the flask "I'm hungry, freezing and damn well exhausted" I have no idea how long we waited outside the scrap yard gate, for we were past caring.

It was then I saw the figure of a man. He walked with a limp, emerging from the area full of skips, smiling and waving his cap. As he moved closer I could hear his voice calling out, in the rhyming dialect of travelling people.

"Good mornin' to ye both" the man said with a welcoming smile. "Ye can leave the wagon there Lad" He gestured to a narrow clearing which lay a short distance beyond the scrap yard gate.

"I'm Adams" he said lifting his cap "And you folks have got to be the people from the hills" Adams helped me climb down the steps from the horsebox. For by now my frozen legs and numb feet seemed to have no connection to my body.

"Come in, come in, and welcome to my abode" Adams said opening the old wooden gate. We followed him past the line of skips, turning right down a narrow pathway. It was here, surrounded by scrap cars where Adams abruptly stopped. Turning towards us, he gave a little bow nodding at what appeared to be three tall stacks of car doors.

"Welcome to my Palace!" He beamed and pointed to the ground, where a line of rubber mats led behind the stacks of metal. The door mats were laid to form a secret pathway which led towards his caravan door. "Ye must be freezing cold" he said watching me shiver "And with nothing warm inside. But we'll soon remedy that we will" Adams threw open the door of his hidden mobile home with a flourish "Follow me into me palace"

Entering Adams home was like finding a treasure trove of gold, which shone from just about everywhere.

He introduced the lady of the palace, who he called either 'Mother' or 'Lass.

"Sit ye down," he said, beckoning to the sofa closest to the warm glowing stove "and drink this tea" he ordered, as he placed large mugs of tea on the table "and if ye wants a drop of something stronger, I'll put some 'fire water' in, so I will." Adams chattered on about his past horses as he poured yet more whisky into his tea.

"Breakfast is served" called Mother, who had stayed in the small kitchen, cooking a breakfast of eggs, bacon and fried bread with toast and homemade marmalade, along with the ever present mugs of tea.

"The most delicious breakfast I've ever had the pleasure of eating," Geoff smiled and looked happy once more. Adams softly talked to himself, but no one listened. He went to sit over by the fire to carry on with his private conversation. I think Mrs. Adams had given up listening long ago. She was a handsome woman with fine bone structure and gave the appearance of a woman with education, decidedly different to Adams. I knew she loved to read by the number of books on the coffee table.

"Reading helps kill the time" she smiled watching me gazing at the books. "My one and only passion" she added "except for Ganador that is."

Glowing with newly found warmth, I started to look at our surroundings. Antique ornaments and hand painted tea sets shone from inside glass fronted display cabinets, all had a predominantly gold theme. The sofas were the color of rich ruby wine, with soft tapestry cushions heavily embroidered in gold thread. On the walls hung photos of horses in gold frames, maybe twenty... almost covering the wooden paneling. Adams had spoken the truth when he said 'come into my palace.' For his home was a haven of splendor, even if it was within the chaos of a scrap yard. When I listened to Adams I could easily see why he irritated Sir Roland when calling at his home every day. I imagined him haggling for the stallion, never taking no for an answer. But he must have done something right, for he got him in the end. In a way he was likeable, but only in small doses. He talked incessantly about his past horses pointing to the photos in gold frames with a driving whip. As the minutes ticked by his speech became slurred... And then I spotted why. Every time he took a sip of tea he poured a drop of whisky into his cup.

"Just to flavor it Lass" He said when he saw me watching.

"Ignore him" said Mother "Drinks his undoing. But tis nothing a mug of strong coffee won't put right" So we waited until the coffee took effect.

Adams was aged around fifty, and still rather handsome. In his younger days he'd probably been somewhat groovy in a dark Gypsy way. He wore new black dealer boots the kind with a little heel, a tweed jacket with a velvet collar, tight black trousers and black open necked shirt. His attire was completed by three dangling neck chains, bracelet and pocket watch, all of gold.

Before very long the coffee took effect and he began to speak of Ganador. He said the name Ganador with admiration, even awe and I listened carefully.

"A God of a horse, wasted with me and the son so he is." Reading between his words made me wonder if all was not well between man and horse. I felt sure the man was having handling problems with the stallion. Maybe it was the number of plasters and bandages covering his fingers that made me suspicious, but then moving scrap metal must also be rough work on the hands "If ye feel warmed through, we'll set out to see Ganador. Follow me, and watch the steps." The rain had stopped, as we followed Adams through a narrow passageway which led into a small area where there was no scrap.

At the bottom of the path he stopped "Ganador's stable," he said proudly. Adams pointed to a ramshackle railway cabin, it stood in a muddy area, close to a small grassless field. Standing next to the railway cabin was a smaller caravan, a shiny new version. To the front of the second caravan I could see a paddock area surfaced with cinders, two water buckets, several driving whips and a few bales of moldy hay.

"So this is Ganador's home" my voice came out almost as a whisper, my heart pounded violently "this is the end of my journey- a railway cabin?"

Suddenly, I felt overwhelmed by events; in a kind of limbo land, wanting so much to see the stallion, yet at the same time fearful of seeing him. Geoff didn't listen to my worries. He walked into the ramshackle cabin with his usual air of quiet confidence.

"He's impressive!" Geoff called from the doorway, before disappearing inside.

"Come in Lass, Ganador's waiting!" Adams beckoned me to enter the stable. When my legs stopped shaking, I slowly walked towards the open doorway.

"Welcome to Ganador's Palace Lass, the Oss won't bite!" Adams took hold of my arm he almost pulled me into the dark cabin.

"Take a look at King Ganador Lass; the finest creature to walk God's earth, so he is"

*

Morning light shimmered through the open doorway casting glittering strips of silver across the stallion's neck. The stallion stood chained to the back wall of the cabin, he looked exactly like a statue. Ganador never moved a muscle, he just stared into my eyes. Arrogance seemed to radiate from him. His superiority was plain for all to see in his oh – so – beautiful eyes. There, amidst the squalor of human rubbish, stood the most magnificent horse I had ever seen.

"Take your time Lass, drink his beauty in, there's no need to hurry"

At that moment I don't think I could have hurried, for I was looking at a horse, through the mists of time. He exactly resembled his forefathers those wild horses of centuries before – and I felt overawed by his grandeur.

I knew immediately that standing before me was a Spanish stallion of the finest blood lines, his statuesque stance and finely chiseled head shouted his superiority. This stallion had no need to be put on show, he knew everyone admired him. He put himself on show just by standing there. His color was shimmering silver, almost ready to turn white, both his mane and tail gleamed like pure silk, a characteristic of the finest Spanish lines. Unfortunately, the mane had been shortened a little, but his tail fell almost to the ground. The stallion's forehand was strikingly handsome, his neck being set on higher than is normal, and though he was measured at sixteen hands he gave the appearance of standing much taller.

Playfully the stallion shook the chain he was tied with swung his head round and fixed me with his penetrating eyes. The kind of eyes that stared directly into mine and for some unknown reason I felt at a loss for words.

"Don't back away Lass" Adams drew still closer to the stallion "Kings can strike terror, just by their eyes, so they can"

"What's this?" I pointed to the stallions left flank… There was a brand; it looked like a crown sitting on a large S, nothing like the usual breeders initials.

"I told you he's a Kings Oss" Adams gazed into my eyes, as he pointed to the mark "And there's his crown to prove it"

Only then did I become conscious of Geoff, who was running his hand along the stallion's back "Pity about his back" Geoff looked inquiringly towards Adams "Any history of accidents, colic or lameness?"

Adams laughed at the stupidity of Geoff's question before replying "Ganador's a strong healthy Oss, so he is" Realizing the futility of his question Geoff carried on with his checks.

"Feel his coat" Adams whispered "Tis like velvet"

"He's thin" replied Geoff from somewhere out of view.

Geoff was correct, his once elegant body was on the verge of being bony and angular, every vertebrae stood out on his top line, like the ridge on a roof. How strange I hadn't noticed this weakness… Just being close to the horse stopped any ability in thinking clearly, I found the stallions charisma overpowering. I didn't wish to hear of his faults, for I knew the horse required months of lunge work, but I didn't care – I'd fallen in love with him – I wanted to take him home.

"Look at his beautiful head and silky mane" Adams pointed to the stallion's head, whilst Ganador watched his every move, patiently waiting for the man to step closer – to come within his reach. He pointed his ears well forwards in a friendly way, but the horse was bluffing, I could see it in his eyes.

"Gaze into his big black beautiful eyes, mysterious, haunting eyes" Adams held out his arm so as to display his goods, and moving a little closer... he pointed. The stallion's expression darkened menacingly. But all was too late... Ganador seized his opportunity; took aim and bit the only remaining unbandaged finger hard. This was a planned move by the stallion, all achieved in a fraction of a second. Adams answered in the only way he knew, by shouting and cursing as he quickly backed away from the horse "What a sod" he cried "What an ungrateful sod" Adams took refuge behind Geoff. Red faced - he nursed his bleeding finger and bruised pride in the comparative safety which lay beyond the reach of Ganador's teeth.

The stallion did not move, he looked satisfied, defiant even. He had struck once more.

# 5. Mark

It was then he whinnied. His call was a greeting whinny, high pitched and bell like, its notes crystal clear. Holding his head high, ears pointed and alert, he carefully listened, his eyes fixed on the stable door. Striking the floor; and shaking the chain he was tied with, the stallion awaited the coming of a friend. This was a sound Ganador wanted to hear.

"What a good lad ye are Mark, coming to help tha' dad" he whined as son Mark walked into the railway cabin.

"He's come to take over as salesman" muttered Geoff "Adams is frightened of the horse."

Mark was smaller than Adams, and darkly handsome in the way of a Romany… his black hair was smoothed down, his eyes were the color of dark rich chocolate. Round his neck he wore a scarlet colored cravat, fastened neatly by a golden tie pin in the shape of a horse's head. Despite his youth, Mark assessed the situation with one short glance and decided on a plan of action. Horses were in his blood, I could see this by how confidently he calmed the stallion.

"Where's me beauty. Where's me lad" he said softly scratching the stallions nose. Ganador responded with soft musical whinnies and Mark pressed his face close to the stallion's awesome head. The horse observed a lack of fear in Adams son and I felt a bond of friendship between them. Quietly yet firmly Mark ordered his father to clean the bleeding finger.

"Get a plaster on it dad, and brew a large pot o' tea" he ordered "These folks have driven from the high hills o' Yorkshire, just to see our Ganador."

"I will son, I will" Adams replied, his voice betrayed relief at this golden opportunity to leave the stallion "I'll be back in a few minutes lad, so I will" he said wearily before making his way back to his caravan.

Mark possessed a certain charm, a charisma and had the likeability factors of a pleasant speaking voice and mischievous wit. His dark eyes were bold and swift... and in a peculiar way his arrogance matched that of Ganador. He delighted in recounting Ganador's antics...

"Every morning at nine I ride him bareback to the shops. We walk up the track and onto the highway, don't we lad..." Mark laughed, and it was then I saw a warm friendly glow enter the stallion's eyes. Maybe it was a look of empathy? "I pick up me fags, and whatever else mother wants. They always have a carrot waiting for Ganador, and all the neighbors stand outside to watch him go by. He's a real proud oss; even the traffic stops to look at 'this' lad!" No doubt Mark felt like a King riding Ganador.... His very own magnificent Spanish stallion - line bred from the bravest battle horses ever to have lived. Maybe Mark doesn't know the history of the breed. But what he's feeling seems to make any knowledge unimportant. Mark and Ganador are inseparable partners and I just wonder if he will ever get over losing the horse? But I'm thinking too far ahead. He's not mine. Will he ever be?

"He's a brave 'oss my Ganador, to be sure, he's a brave lad" he said proudly "If we're away for the day we let the 'oss patrol the yard. Any thing strange and he's there, better than a guard dog this lad is" Mark brushed the stallions coat once more.

"Is Ganador trained as a guard horse?" I stared at Mark in total disbelief "But horses don't guard..."

"Some do Lady!" Shaking his head vigorously, Mark laughed at my lack of knowledge "And this lad's 'silent,' he's not like a dog with all that barking." he said gleefully "Protects his territory, so he does, like it's in his blood. Should anyone be creeping about, this lad corners them until we get back, frightens them to death, don't you Lad. Ganador holds them, has them as good as snared, you should see him on duty, his ears flat back, teeth flashing - and if they try to run for it, he's quicker than they are. Stands up on his hind legs and blocks them with his body" Mark claimed proudly, amidst peals of laughter, and I had no hesitation in feeling that his stories about Ganador were true. Marks dark eyes looked back at me steadily in a way that reminded me how little I knew about the horse. Did I even want to know? I tried not to ask. Maybe I was frightened of what he might say. But then the words just came tumbling out

"Has he ever hurt anyone?" I didn't intend to speak. What's happened in the past has been and gone. Please don't tell me he's a dangerous stallion, because I don't want to know, but I think Mark wants to tell me. Thank goodness Geoff's not listening. So I watched Marks face carefully – there's no sign of him holding anything back "When I say hurt, I mean has he ever savaged anyone… Has he tasted blood?"

"Surely not" he sounded amused "But thieves don't come complaining, do they now… Ganador saves all his savaging for Dad, so he does!"

Once again the rain sailed down, the ash covered paddock and tracks across the scrap yard were now unrecognizable. "Horrible weather," he said "the grounds taking a drink, but spring is on its way" For a moment Mark contemplated this fact, probably thinking of a spring without Ganador.

"Why not take a real good look at him? I'll be off to find Dad and the tea." Geoff stroked the stallions neck, before beginning the all important checks on Ganador's legs. The hocks, stifles and fetlocks would be carefully checked for any evidence of filling or heat. The tell tale signs of old injuries.

"Nice clean legs" he said, running his fingers slowly upwards towards the suspect back. He pressed down hard on each protruding vertebrae in turn, but the stallion showed little interest and no discomfort.

"Back injuries have a nasty habit of returning" Geoff looked at me hard "You understand the risk then?"

Of course I understood the risk. It was a risk no sensible person would take, but I'd fallen in love with this horse.

"Please give him a chance" I closed my eyes and held back the worry that's emerging fast "What's the very worst that could happen?"

"Progressive unsoundness in the hind quarters…most usually in the hock… impossible to work without a healthy engine. What do you want to do?"

"Take him home… give him a chance"

"Ganador's high in the order of buying risks, very high indeed…" My heart sank as he said this "But if his hooves are good then he's worth a bid"

For a while the horse stood quietly, sometimes rattling the chains which held him captive, now and then pretending to hear a sound in the far distance or calling to an imaginary sweetheart with a soft yet ringing whinny. I held my breath as he carefully examined the hooves, knowing this was a test Ganador could not fail. Being a blacksmith had made Geoff wary of poor hoof quality and he firmly believed in the old saying 'no foot, no horse.'

"Good open feet, sound and tough, I know it's only March, but he's got the best feet I've seen this year."

At this point I began to breathe more easily, one down and only two to go, he was almost mine. So we made the decision right there, inside that ramshackle cabin.

"It's a yes then" Geoff smiled "I must be a fool"

"What if the gypsy wants more money than we've got to offer?"

"Leave it to me" So I left it with Geoff.

At that exact moment Adams entered the cabin with the promised mugs of tea, his injured finger now covered with a plaster, he looked across to Geoff and said,

"What do ye think of him Lad?" Adams voice was cautious yet controlled "If ye likes the lad, we'll get round the table" I love him I wanted to say, but I couldn't let Adams know that. It was almost time to make our lowest offer, find a few things wrong with the horse, try not to anger the man, pay and go… Or so I thought. After drinking the all important mugs of tea, we followed Adams back to his caravan to complete the deal. I sat close to the warm stove, entirely unprepared for what was to come.

"We all stand round the table lass" he said patiently "It's time for our little ceremony." Pouring himself a large glass of whisky he firmly took my arm, and directed me towards the table.

"Try to be more upbeat" Geoff whispered "And smile"

But I can't find the energy to smile. How can I possibly be upbeat when I don't understand what the hell's going on? He could be setting us up. I mean handing cash over inside a Gypsies caravan is not in any sensible persons rule book. Is it? He could say he'd changed his mind about the sale, refuse to accept Geoff's offer, keep the deposit. There were plenty of obstacles in the way just yet. And until Ganador was in the horsebox, Adams held the ace card. I didn't know one person who'd be cheerful in this situation, except Geoff.

"We travelling people have a custom, a gentlemen's practice, so it is" Adams placed a whisky bottle in the center of the table, and lined four glasses up. "This is how travelling people do business. It's so we all know where we stand... Put them in the picture Mark Lad"

"Geoff begins by shouting his lowest bid" Mark said obligingly "And then we're off! The biddings over when Geoff stops slapping, so it is, for good or bad - richer or poorer." So this is how Gypsies buy and sell? There's no receipt book, just whisky and a price arrived at by slapping hands. Geoff will never forgive me.

"If I buy him at the right price I'll be happy" Geoff said in a grim voice.

"The lad reached eight thousand at Appleby, the crowd went mad about Ganador" Mark smiled, he looked amused "They were clapping and cheering, never seen such a magnificent oss" When he said Appleby I turned my face away hoping Geoff had not seen my surprised look... Could it be that Ganador and the Gypsy horse were one and the same? If he was the same, did it matter? There was no point in reliving history, maybe angering Adams. At this moment in time I had a slim chance of buying this mystery horse, of removing him from haggling Gypsy's and scrap yards for good. I had fallen in love with this creature from the past. I wanted Ganador more than anything in life... And I was determined to have him.

"Well he won't be reaching a fraction of that today. Horses don't grow younger" said Geoff sharply.

And so we stood in a circle around that table, Geoff facing Adams - I opposite Mark, and within moments, our initiation into this Romany ritual was set in motion.

# 6. Romany Ritual

In true gypsy spirit Geoff started the sale off with a very low offer.

"Eight pound bid" Called out Geoff. Adams muttered something but then slapped Geoff's hand.

"Make it eight thousand and we might do business" shouted Adams.

"Make it eight hundred and not a penny more"

"He's a class stallion" shrieked Adams "the oss has the breeding of a King"

Slowly Geoff raised his bid, in the time honored way of travelling men by agreeing, not with a pen, nor a vet but simply the slap of a hand.

The bidding went on, the slapping got faster.

"Do you want to keep him?" Geoff called his final price "Final price is eighteen hundred"

"I'll keep the oss" retorted Adams.

For most of the time I'd no idea what was going on, I don't think Geoff understood either. My mind kept on replaying the awful possibilities that could still happen before the stallion was safely in the box. Anything could take place, until this Romany ritual thing was out of the way. I just wanted to get him away from there, as far away as possible, if and when we got past the remaining obstacles.

Sighing wearily, Geoff tried to negotiate his way through the perils of Romany style horse trading. This was not his forte, it was unfamiliar territory and he watched Adams carefully. After slapping hands, Adams and Mark would shout, sometimes in a strange rhyming dialect, one I did not recognize. Maybe it's the talk of the Romany people? Whenever Adams holds up his right hand, we feel obliged to do the same.

"But we're givin' the oss away, so we are" the men excitedly shouted. The slapping and shouting appeared to follow a definite pattern, a technique the two men knew exceedingly well. At last Geoff shouts his final offer.

"Closing bid two thousand. Say no and keep the horse" suddenly there was a hesitant silence. Being hopeless at deciphering this unspoken message, I desperately glanced towards Mark.

"Time to put a little cash on the table Geoff" confided Mark. He winked and patted his back pocket "It's time to show the money, so it is."

Begrudgingly, Geoff counted out a small deposit…

"Ten per cent equals two hundred" The hand slapping became more rapid, the shouting louder. The whole world seemed to stand still. Geoff counted out the deposit in twenties.

"The remaining cash when he's in the box"

"May luck go with him" Adams cried out. And I knew Ganador was almost ours! When the noise, which Adams and Mark delighted in, had died down, coffee cups were placed over by the stove.

"May the oss and his new owner have good health," Adams toasted Ganador, and then Geoff before sitting down.

At this point I became aware of Mother; she's quietly sobbing and tears are running down her cheeks. She's worried about something… I hope it's not Ganador. After blowing her nose and wiping steam from her glasses she speaks of her fears, her voice is filled with passion, her eyes look into mine.

"My proud Ganador" she pays no attention to her tears, her voice is choked and full of emotion "He's a real gentleman. He's been a good friend to me. I want you to promise me something lass" She stares into my eyes, I try to stay calm, but with increasing difficulty. It becomes clearer by the second that Mother doesn't want him to go. Why had I never imagined that Mother might be a problem?

"I'm sure Ganador will be happy" I force a smile and try to think of something reassuring to say "We have a stable and a field ready for Ganador" But she doesn't listen, she's too upset.

"My proud Ganador" she repeats "There will never be another Ganador, never" suddenly I feel so guilty. Only a minute ago I wanted to take him away, as far away as possible, now I feel responsible for causing her tears.

"Every morning at ten, I make Ganador a cup of tea. He drinks from a china cup, and takes milk with two sugar lumps" The two men nodded in agreement

"When Mark turns him into the yard, so as to clean his bed, Ganador makes his way to the caravan. He knocks on the door with his nose and waits for his cup of tea. And by the way, he doesn't drink like a horse, he drinks like we do" Mother said.

"So he does, he does" Adams and Mark said together.

"The horse drinks just like we do" they repeated.

"He sips his cup of tea, just like a gentleman, it's the highlight of his day" Mother begged me to continue with the stallions treat, his daily cup of tea "To his dying day Lass"

And to his dying day Ganador took tea each morning, with milk and two sugars, and Mother was correct Ganador didn't drink like a horse, he sipped his tea, just like a King.

Geoff looked at his watch, most probably thinking of the lengthy drive back to the hills of Yorkshire.

"If we load him now, we may get back before midnight" he said "with a bit of luck on the weather front, that is" Geoff added optimistically.

"Park up close to the caravans" Mark ordered "Good strong hard core, it is" Once parked, he jumps out and drops the ramp. Geoff's decided he's only paying Adams when Ganador's safely inside the box. For he knows the stallion may be suspicious, he could refuse to load. What if Adams wants the money now, before Ganador's loaded? Geoff will say no. Maybe he'll get mad, change his mind and threaten to drive away without the horse. But I'm definite he will never pay the money over, until Ganador is in the box, until he's ours.

Mark led Ganador from the railway cabin to the ramp, but the stallion had other ideas, he decided he did not want to enter the horsebox. He reared high into the air and splattered a spray of wet ash over all who stood there. All four of us were plastered in thick black dirt. The Gypsy looked ever so mad.

"Arrogant sod of an oss" Adams shouted angrily, shaking his fist in the direction of the stallion. I had never seen anyone who looked quite so mad. He's covered in mud. I can't see his face, only his scowl. It had to be the whisky - it caused some people to lose control.

For a few seconds, all is quiet except the rain which lashed down, hammering on the empty oil drums in loud drips. Ganador seemed frozen to the spot and refused to move either forwards or backwards. Adams never moved, his face looked like thunder, his anxiety plain to see. Maybe the prospect of not getting his money and having to keep the stallion had all become too much. Ganador was winning the battle between the Gypsy, his fingers and entering the horsebox.

Adams looked to be thinking about what he could do next. He glanced at his driving whip. Geoff walked over to him and told him to 'calm down man' but he didn't listen, he's fuming.

Quite suddenly his temper snapped, picking up his longest driving whip he ran towards the horse shouting "Sod of a creature ye are, a sod" Mark blocked his father, and swiftly removed the whip from his hand.

"Quiet Dad" he said "the oss is upset. Stand o'er there" He pointed towards Mother who sheltered inside the caravan door "Keep Dad quiet Mother, brew some tea, give him a whisky or two" pleaded Mark. He handed the driving whip safely over to Geoff. By now, everyone on or near the paddock was soaking wet and filthy. Ganador's frantic pawing had tested every ones temper. As the drama played out, the rain continued to fall fast and unremittingly. It seemed wetter than the moors, something I had always thought impossible. The ash paddock had disappeared; it must be under the black mud and floating paper waste.

"It's all been too much for the old man" Mark confided, calmly feeding the stallion a carrot before walking him to the ramp once more.

The stallion hesitated at the entry to the box, he called out once, but the smell of bran got the better of him.  At his own speed he walked up the ramp and into his stall. He had a strange superiority that made his entrance dignified, every step every movement appeared to be ruled by his all pervading confidence, or whatever else it was that made him different from a normal horse. Ganador had proved beyond doubt that 'He' had made the decision… Not us.

"Get that ramp up and quick" Adams ordered Mark, but he did no such thing. Instead he came to Ganador, and stroked the stallion's neck for the last time.

"Be a good lad for these nice folks, won't ye Ganador, me beauty" he said in a sad empty voice before jumping down. Pushing the ramp shut with a loud clang, he locked it firmly. It was then I heard Mother weeping she cried out in a wail of distress, the stallion had been a good friend to her, possibly her only friend.

Adams attempted to conceal his smile, but I saw it in his eyes, they were glinting with happiness. Finally he was set free from his trials by the stallion. Now he could relax. As every minute passed the horse was nearer to departing, the money all but in his hand.

He strolled to the ramp and pressed a large envelope into my hands, the words 'bill of sale' were written on the back of the package, but really I think he's here just to watch Geoff counting out money. When Geoff had done counting, Adams hurriedly grasped the money and handed it over to Mark for a recount.

"Count the money careful like son" he said gleefully. Marks index finger moved at the speed of light, he must be well practiced in this particular skill.

"That man Roland from the big house sent this package down only last night" Adams said cautiously "Ganador's papers are in it, he wants you to have his Pedigree" he smiled "Only lives close by, he does. Gardener came down saying he's to post the rest next week." Inside the envelope were three neatly folded certificates, the language is Spanish. All were hand written in the neatest scroll I had ever seen. The Stallions State Registration Papers, identity and his long Pedigree. I'm overwhelmed, but try not to show my feelings, carefully placing the package inside my coat pocket.

"Weathers taking up" said Geoff staring up at the sky. The

heavy rain had turned to drizzle, with snatches of blue amongst the grey of the clouds. "Time to be on our way" he said, already thinking of future weather conditions on the moorland road. Black ice, impenetrable mist even blizzards were more common than uncommon during the month of March over the high moors of Yorkshire. I hugged mother and shook hands with Adams and then Mark. Father and son stood together like soldiers on parade and a wave of guilt flooded over me for not having trusted them more.

"Don't forget his tea lass" she said still weeping "He's more than just a horse, better than we are, he is" I nodded my head in silent understanding and squeezed her hand.

"Ye be home 'afore midnight" Adams said, clearly not understanding the ways of the moors.

Mark walked over to the cab to say farewell.

"You've got yourself a real beauty Geoff" he said "I'll miss him, so I will"

Geoff started up the engine, driving through the gate and onto the muddy track. Adams waved his cap, Mark and Mother turned away.

"God speed ye journey home" Adams shouted.

And so we began the long drive home, back to the hills of Yorkshire, with Ganador V our Spanish stallion.

# 7. Journey Home

*March 14. 1980.*

"Thank you… and goodbye!" I called through the open window. Geoff drove away from the confines of the scrap yard and up the litter covered track where even the bushes wore coverings of paper waste.

"I don't know what you're thanking that scoundrel Adams for" Geoff said heatedly before turning left at the white painted sign "He squeezed an extra three hundred quid out of me – said I clapped at the wrong time, he wouldn't back down… What could I say?"

"Nothing really, he wasn't the type to listen - Mother was a sweet lady though. I still feel guilty about feeling so suspicious. After all they made us welcome, didn't they?"

"They were friendly people. But I will never forget the…"

"Three hundred pounds" I said weakly, knowing it was all my fault "Put it down to being unfamiliar in the rules of Romany horse trading…" Almost immediately we passed a row of shabby, unpainted houses. The row of houses stood between The White Horse Inn and a small shop, probably the same one Mark rode to every morning to 'get his fags'- where they always had a carrot waiting for Ganador. Even the fields had an uncared for expression, fenced with rusty barbed wire and dilapidated wooden posts. A few poor looking cows stood in corners of these enclosed areas as though for shelter, but standing deep in mud and misery. The kind of misery, extremes of weather bring to all animals with little food and no shelter.

Our journey so far was uneventful Ganador munched his hay or stood quietly. I suppose the stallion had finally accepted the inevitability of his fate as all animals do in the end. He was being moved, and where to, he did not know. Perhaps he would end his journey in a knackers' yard, or with a new owner, passed on like baggage. The stallion could not speak therefore he must accept the will of humans.

Still the rain poured down. The horsebox made a regular 'whoosh' splashing sound as it passed over holes and puddles in the damaged road surface. Soon we were driving on the brightly lit motorway, where any trace of poverty could melt away into the prosperous world of concrete structures, smooth roads, neon lit signs, and large restaurants. We felt no urge to hurry, stopping at every lorry driver's café to offer Ganador water, fill up his hay net or clean his stall. At each stop I redid his rug and then stroked his silken mane. I couldn't stop feeling thrilled every time I looked at him. I felt like a child with a new toy. The stallion began to whinny softly whenever Geoff approached him, meaning Geoff was now accepted.

"Feels good to be going home," Geoff sighed, he sounded relieved "with yet one more addition to the family... Our very own guard horse. I never thought I'd be silly enough to buy a horse without seeing him move - and one of uncertain temperament" he gave me one of his critical, sideways glances "As well as buying him from gypsies... and seeing my three hundred quid go down the drain" I knew Geoff would never get over his loss, after all he was a Yorkshire man. He firmly believed in looking after his money.

"Blame it all on me"

"I will.... What have we got to eat?"

Fortunately Mother had insisted on filling our flasks with coffee and packing the empty sandwich containers with delicious home baked cakes. She was very kind. Why had I thought of her as an obstacle, when she only wanted Ganador's happiness? To Mother the stallion had been a special friend, an acquaintance she could trust. He knocked on her door, every morning at ten, to say hello. She probably enjoyed the ritual of making tea each morning, in delicate china cups. And the stallion had valued 'Mothers' friendship greatly, for he understood he must sip his tea, so as not to damage the china she held to his lips. And as she said 'the highlight of Ganador's day is having tea with me'. It was probably the highlight of hers too. The stallion and Mother had been the best of friends, and I had made her a promise, a promise I would keep.

I'm not quite sure how I expected to feel when we left the yard. But what I did not know was that the images of the travellers and chaos of the scrap yard would stay etched in my memory. I would never forget them, never. I had been dazzled by the brightness of their world, so rich with colorful people. Despite surroundings of scrap and waste, the travellers living abode was that of a palace, warm and golden. But it was a world I could only visit as a stranger, a world with its own rules, laws and customs, all shrouded in the mists of secrecy. Their generosity had been undeniable. We had been welcomed as guests in a golden palace, a palace that cost Geoff three hundred pounds to visit, plus the cost of Ganador. I would always remember them, the warmth of Mother, young handsome Mark, who charmed me with his Gaelic gaiety. I would never forget his jet black curls, nor his blood red cravat... held together by a gold pin in the shape of a horse's head. Mark's genuine fondness for the stallion was indisputable, as was the stallions bond with Mark. And yet Adams possessed a confusing trait, he appeared friendly and jovial on the outside but underneath this bluff the stallion felt a weakness in Adams and decided he did not admire it. The horse detested him, and worked steadily towards infuriating the man by destroying Adams pride. This is the way of highly bred horses. Any affection the gypsy once felt towards the stallion was now gone. He wished only for the horse to be taken away, far far away, so that he could gather up his pride, and what he now knew to be false confidence. Next time he bought a horse he would be sure never to buy a 'class' horse ever again.

To pass the time, I read and reread his incredible lineage... his ancestor's sound like they are out of history books. The stallion – I mean Ganador is a work of art, a horse from the past; the experience of owning him has got to feel similar to that of an art collector who discovers a 'Renoir' or 'Van Gogh.' To me, finding

Ganador is an incomparable feeling. One of the Worlds last battle horses, found in a Gypsies scrap yard. True life can be a lot stranger than fiction.

After many hours driving on straight and perfect roads it's time to lookout for the slip road signaling our departure from the motorway, the second step of our journey home.

The black of night is already upon us, there are no stars, just darkness, probably because of the heavy rains. We pull off the motorway and make our way towards the mill towns of Lancashire. Slowly the horsebox lumbers along on the forever twisting and turning valley roads.

Gradually, the landscape of mill chimneys and rows of terraced houses changes to that of open fields with small farms. I suppose the farms once supplied the needs of the town by delivering milk and eggs, but the supermarkets have taken over. Small farms aren't needed, so they have all been sold as barn conversions or holiday homes.

The only farms left are factory farms, and they are hidden away from the public's gaze. I try not to think of the animals in factory farms, never seeing the light of day, incarcerated and then packaged for super market shelves. Thank goodness 'intensive' farms have no wish to set up on the moors, as yet.

After the towns we drive through the outer reaches of suburbia, small quant country villages with restaurants and Pubs. The cottages are radiant with the glow of lanterns and soft window lights. The villages seem to be clustered in sheltered areas, close to the towns but surrounding the moor.

"What sensible places to live" Geoff mutters. I gaze out at the manicured lawns, carefully sited trees and boundaries of neat, perfect hedges, with not a twig out of place.

At the 'Crooked Billet Inn' Geoff stops and places a thick woollen blanket under the stallion's day rug. I start getting blankets and sleeping bags ready for the final part of the journey over the moor. It's always possible for double figured temperature falls on the moorland road. Anything and everything is possible on the Yorkshire moors. It's a world so very different to the towns in the valley and we prepare for the worst weather the moor can possibly throw at us… for daring to cross its territory.

Whenever the box halts, the stallion whinnies; they are beautiful cries from his heart, not loud, but deep and intense. I had never heard such soft throaty whickers before; both melodious and vibrant, the sound brought glorious music to my ears and tears to my eyes. Almost home, and I still can't believe he's mine. Only hours now and then we are home. I can feel a stillness closing in. The sounds of living have gone away, its quiet now. At a certain point on the road, the strangest thing always happens. Suddenly there's total silence, it falls like a cloak. I can hear myself breathing. It feels like entering another world. I don't know why, but the hush never fails to surprise me. It's like being in a bubble, so peaceful and still. As the periphery of the moor starts to close in around us, I can sense mile after mile of wilderness. Villages and civilization have no place out here. The landscape is only recognizable by far apart lonely looking dwellings which stand on the moors edge. When the last tree has disappeared, and the sound of the wind howls in the distance, I know we're in the rough country. Dry stone walls now take the place of hedges, more often than not broken and crumbling. Nothing much survives on the moor, even stone perishes on falling to the ground. At the roadside rocks and fallen stones glisten with slimy freezing mist, always a warning of black ice ahead.

There is a steaming mist surrounding the top of the moors, and as we drive higher it shuts out everything, but for a few meters of road. As we drive further the swirling mist becomes thicker, the cold more intense and biting, but at last the rain stops. Everything visible by our headlights sparkles with crisp ice crystals. Ice is a winter hazard on the old stagecoach road. It's called black ice and sometimes the wheels start to slide, it makes the road feel like a skating rink. But new tarmac surfaces and grit do not seem to be a priority for moorland roads "Too remote, no one lives out there" or so the council decided. I wonder if the council has ever visited the top of the moors, probably not.

The time is almost midnight when Geoff pulls onto the last road, it's very narrow and this is the road which leads to Toby Jug Farm, or 'home.' The inky blackness of this old stagecoach route always surprises me, and though we know every crack and hole by now, it's a road that has to be treated with caution. Moving at a snail's pace he tries to keep the horsebox away from bumps and holes. The road is unlit; it's also covered in ice and full of potholes. After reaching the highest point of the moor, he pulls into a lay - by and calls Sue.

"Nearly home" Geoff sounds completely spent. "I'm putting the wheel chains on." He leaves the engine running and puts the heater full on trying to find enough energy to face the sub zero temperatures and biting wind outside. Moorland cold is different to any other cold, it has to be experienced to know just how different. Dragging the chains from the cab, he wrapped the light chain round the front wheels. After two minutes outside, he climbs back into the warmth of the cab and waits for some feeling to return into his frozen fingers.

With no time to waste, he starts up the engine, for the final part of our journey home. I don't know why, but the mist seems to be falling even lower. It's clinging to the ice on the road, taken a different shape, low and crawling, floating and rippling like steam vapor hiding the roads many dangers.

"Black ice… good job the chains are on" Slippery pools of deadly black ice lay in wait on the unlit road, with frozen tentacles crawling over the roads surface. Like shining silver snakes coiling and twisting in the broken tarmac. After a few minutes we're ready for the short descent, and the end of our journey.

In the distance lamps are glowing from outside the 'Shepherds Rest,' the moors pub, where long ago stagecoaches changed horses, and where history was written inside every stone.

Shortly after one a.m. we turn down the narrow lane leading to home. The yard lights are on, ready for his arrival, bright, welcoming lights that sparkle on the frost covered cobbles.

"Feels good to be on home ground" Geoff immediately sounds some way to becoming his former self "Let the side ramp down when I knock" he rapidly disappears through the grooms door which leads into Ganador's quarters. He will tap his usual signal to indicate when he wants the ramp lowered. This is our way of communicating when in the back of a horsebox. Shouting only spooks a horse. Immediately, my exhaustion starts to lift. I feel so happy!

"What does he look like?" the friendly voice of Sue calls out, from somewhere in the stables "I'm so excited!"

"He's beautiful Sue" I reply "Incredibly beautiful."

"You followed your dream girl!" she said laughing "Some call it the luck of the draw, but I think its destiny" Geoff knocks twice which means he is ready to unload Ganador... Sue helps me to slowly drop the side ramp.

We stood transfixed, watching the lights converge upon the stallion's outline.

His magnificent figure stood motionless at the top of the ramp, the silken hair of his mane and tail gently lifting in the breeze. When his eyes had adjusted to the bright light, he signaled his intentions to proceed, by striking the wooden floor with his hoof. The sound was like thunder in the quiet of the night. Hesitating for an instant, he looked from right to left, before breathing in the fresh moorland air and the smell of new horses. Then, he screamed his most powerful stallion calls, the sound echoed over moor and valley, with a message to all other horses that 'he' Ganador had arrived. It was a glorious sound, vibrant and at the same time majestic. His calls could be heard echoing over the high moor and deep into the valley below.

Geoff stepped onto the ramp; and the stallion followed, dancing down into the stable yard with the highest of steps. Holding his head proudly, he paraded in passage as he passed by our five other horses, greeting each with a soft melodious whinny.

The resident horses knew there was something very different about this visiting stranger. All stood alert and wide eyed, like children staring at Christmas lights. Every eye, all ten of them, looked on in wonder, watching and listening to his every movement. His exit from the horsebox and his walk to the stable had shown a talent in stage management. He had displayed his great superiority, every breath and every step he took reminded me that here was no ordinary mortal horse. Here was the horse line bred through the centuries to be the battle horse of Kings, selected for his skills in combat and displayed for prestige. The horse painted by famous artists, and carved by sculptors to depict the peak of beauty and nobility. Here was the horse that founded the principles of classical equitation, who had known the splendors of Ancient Greece and Rome.

For a moment, Sue appeared to be frozen to the spot.

"I've never seen such a beautiful horse" she whispered, her eyes wide with wonderment. Ganador calmly walked into his loosebox, he stood quietly allowing Sue to change his travelling sheet and place a feed in his manger. Then he turned, singing out the most beautiful whinny I had ever heard, and only at that moment did he begin to eat. A great thrill of pride welled up inside me. This was the moment I had longed for, what I had dreamed about for seven long years. . . Ganador had arrived.

*'His neigh is like the bidding of a monarch and his countenance enforces homage.'*
*William Shakespeare.*

# 8. Yorkshire Moors.

*Toby Jug Farm March 15 1980*

Toby Jug Farm stood almost at the very top of the moors, high above the pretty village of Heptonstall in the county of North Yorkshire. It was built in the seventeenth century, 1616 to be precise, had hand carved mullioned windows and huge stone fireplaces. Many families had passed through its doors. How many had died there was anybody's guess. They died young according to the head stones in the graveyard. There was a scattering of maybe twenty farms, a local pub called the Shepherds Rest and a 17 C graveyard within the moorland hamlet of Moonraker Heights.

Nearly all the other farms were strung out along the high narrow road, and were accessible only by rough, deeply rutted soil tracks that climbed over the horizon to the uninhabited spread of the open moors. The inner stretch of moors was remote and unfriendly; sometimes it could be frightening, forgotten by walkers, ignored by local farmers. A place where it was usually raining and cold, with the threat of a storm never far away, and the regular howling of a wind, somewhere in the distance. The local sheep farmers, called the open moor 'the ocean,' a place to keep well away from with its many bogs, sudden storms, and freezing winds.

At the top of our farm track, overlooking the road was a sober reminder of a time long ago, the 17 century graveyard. It stood in a triangular shaped plot, with high stone walls, and contained about forty beautifully carved headstones. All the headstones leaned over in a westerly direction, some almost to the ground. But on every headstone was carved out a delightful line of prose. Within these high walls, lay the remains of almost the entire Moonraker Heights 17 c community. Whole families buried in the same small graves; from little Joe just one year to grandfather Jonah, all of seventy nine years, Bubonic Plague having taken them all.

Along past the graveyard stood the Shepherds Rest Inn, or local pub, where neighboring sheep farmers gathered in the evening's to exchange gossip, ridicule the ministry or amuse any passing tourists. Moorland farmers spoke without any familiarities, in a dialect known only to them, containing many strange words and phrases. The farmers delighted in their ability to act out and perform their role in life, often with Oscar winning performances. The Shepherds Rest was a place where strangers quickly became friends, and where there was nowhere better in England, to enjoy the company of such warm, friendly people.

Toby Jug Farm stood in two differing worlds. To the back existed the wilderness of the high open moors, and to the front was a valley, a very beautiful valley. The farmland sloped gently downwards, in a patchwork quilt of semi- moorland fields, and was entirely cut off, but for one footpath. In the hollow of the valley stood a cavernous rocky gorge where the mountain birds sheltered in winter, perching on perilous ledges carved into the rock.

A river ran through the foot of the gorge, with green fertile sides. Moisture from the river filled the banks with ferns, mosses and wild rhododendron bushes, which were almost as tall as the few half dead trees. In the distance loomed the majestic high hills and crags of North Yorkshire, towering over the valley, shading the pasture with strips of gold then lavender light throughout the months of spring then summer.

The farm land was divided into three fields, all sloping downwards to a meadow, where the hares ran free. Fragile moorland grassland grew amongst tiny delicate flowers within the meadow, four dry stone walls enclosing its boundaries sheltering it from the moorland winds. The meadow was not high and windswept like the three fields but soft rich and green, with a sparkling stream running through it, winding down to the river that flowed through the gorge.

Originally the place had been a row of six weaver's cottages, with a large central barn. Three cottages stood either side of the barn looking like two book stands. The farm house consisted of the three larger cottages each with adjoining door, the stables the three smaller. Each loose box had once served as a living kitchen or sitting room, and possessed a hand carved stone fireplace, door step and original stone mullioned windows. The floors of the back looseboxes or sitting rooms were paved in large stone flags which continued to a footpath that led up the farm track past the graveyard then out over the moors.

At the end of the row of stables was an alleyway, which led into the old carriage room. Inside the carriage room were four rounded corners, lots of space, plenty of height and two minute mullioned windows.

We called this appendage the tack room, storing saddles, grooming equipment, and horse food inside its splendid façade. Ganador's loose box was to be the large living kitchen, next to the alley way which looked into the stable yard and over the valley.

The morning following Ganador's arrival dawned freezing cold and miserably dark, with a howling wind moving in from the moors. The high Yorkshire moors seldom gave any indication of changing weather conditions. Often, in less than one hour a calm winter's day would be transformed into a raging storm, with winds strong enough to blow a man over.

"Siberian winds" said Geoff blowing on his fingers "Low and strong, like a wall of ice"

Sue groaned and shivered "Look at that snow filled sky" she said "The new horse must be wondering where the hell he's come to. Why does it always have to snow before my long weekend?" Sue sighed, pulling on her third pair of socks. She hated moorland winters, growing up in a more sheltered part of Leeds had softened her, or so Geoff thought.

"Rubbish" replied Geoff "This place has got to feel like paradise, compared to spending his days looking at a wall in a scrap yard." Geoff began to butter his sixth slice of toast, moving the marmalade within close proximity to his plate.

"Norma" grumbled Sue "He's playing chess with the marmalade jar." Sue swiftly moved the jar into the middle of the table "Check mate" said an irritated Sue, calling a halt to Geoff's little game. Geoff and Sue had already seen to the horses, de-iced water buckets and gritted several paths, having been down in the stable yard from the early hour of seven a.m.

Geoff sounded pleased with our new stallion, and I thanked my lucky stars Ganador had remained on his best behavior, at least for his first day. Let it long continue I thought, hopefully crossing my fingers, with Sir Roland's warnings ever present in my mind.

"How can we exercise him in this wind?" asked Sue listening to the unsettling roaring of the wind as the high gusts slammed into the window panes.

"We can't" replied Geoff "Clanging and banging doesn't make for happy horses. He'd be terrified down in the school"

The school was our small indoor arena, complete with gallery and one, enormous mirror. When we first moved into the farm Geoff had decided that his number one priority was the building of an indoor riding school, closely followed by new stone roofing over house and barn. Although I disagreed with him at the time, the indoor school had quickly become my idea of paradise, and I couldn't imagine life without it, not with the threat of serious weather never far from the door.

At eleven a.m. I fought my way down to the stables, in lashing hailstones and what must have been a hundred mile per hour wind. For a few moments I stood silently, enjoying watching the horses, and the everyday activities of all stable yards. Sue was grooming Ganador, and Geoff shoeing Donovan, his 17 hands beloved Irish gelding.

Any concerns I'd had about the stallion's temperament, or temper, were quickly running out of steam. Ganador was immediately gentle and kind towards his neighbors in the stable block… neither had he threatened Sue, she was in his box grooming him. The other horses appeared fascinated by this strange creature from foreign lands, relaxed and happy in his presence. They watched him closely, mesmerized by his swift graceful movements and musical whinnies, his every action followed by curious inquiring interest. When he whinnied, they listened, if he stood with his head over the door, so did they. Undoubtedly Ganador was now Leader, and had received that honor with dignity, for was this not his role in life?

Every movement he made, every singing, reverberating whinny, contained that touch of aristocracy, which was haughty, proud yet inimitably noble. Ganador reminded me that here was a creature born to be a King, and for a few minutes I stood quietly, watching his every movement.

Sue brushed rhythmically, in time to the thumping beat from her radio, which stood on the window ledge.

"Pow-er-ful" she said, allowing the syllables of the word to follow the rhythm of the music "Been at number one for three weeks now"

Sue continued brushing steadily to the thudding beat "They all think so too" she added defensively, nodding towards the horses, who surprisingly did appear to be listening attentively.

"Who am I to argue against popular demand?" I said patiently, refusing to be drawn on the merits of this week's number one, when my personal idea of heaven; was to be lulled by a Mozart Concerto, or pacified with the strains of Bach's Cantata's. Sue and Geoff considered me a lost cause, on the subject of popular music. According to some, I was a 'classical snob'... But what did they expect from a trained musician? Classical music had formed the backbone of my life; there was nowhere nearer heaven than when perfectly ordered rhythm and technical ability came together. It had the same qualities as a highly trained horse. Maybe that's why I felt passionate about both.

"What's this Norma?" Sue pointed to his brand.

"It's a crown"

"I've never seen a horse with a crown on his flank"

"Well you have now- The Gypsy told me it was a royal crown"

She stepped back to examine her grooming, then pointed to

three strange black marks, which stared out from beneath the stallion's winter coat.

"Exposed under his winter coat" said Sue in a dramatic tone of voice "What are they?"

Ganador was beginning to lose his warm winter coat in patches, and to reveal areas of a sleek summer coat, the color of shimmering silver. But plain to see were two large spur scars on his girth line, and a wide bridle scar, running behind his ears. The scars were a dull black color, and had once been open wounds, ugly symbols of some mans violence, where his shining silver coat would never grow again.

"Scars" I said with a grimace "Old scars, most probably inflicted by his breaker"

"You mean he's been roughed up?" quizzed Sue, turning towards me.

"Some call rough treatment breaking, sad but true."

The scars told a story, Ganador had been made to suffer pain in the hands of his breaker, or as Ganador remembered, in the hands of a man, and a horse possessing his spirit never would forget this fact. For all time he would be prepared to draw upon the agony of his painful memories. Horses never forget pain or violence; this is the way of the horse, the important x factor that has made sure of his survival from the times of pre history.

"We can't expect a horse of his quality, and bought from the world of a scrap yard, not to throw up a few surprises, now can we?" I said, wondering what other surprises the horse would yet reveal.

"You worry for the world Norma" said Sue absently, as she picked out then measured Ganador's unshod feet. "Can't repeat history, what's done is done" she added with all the unseeing finality of youth. "Don't suppose we will ever know the true story of Ganador" she added, checking the measurements once again "But it does sound like a fairy story, finding a horse like him, stabled in a shed, in the middle of a scrap yard, and with Gypsies?"

Sue called out the measurements to Geoff who stood waiting outside the loosebox door. "13-7 front shoes and 13-5 backs" I watched Geoff scribble the numbers onto the back of his hand, paper not being allowed when the forge was lit, before disappearing into the quiet of his blacksmiths workplace.

"Guess what?" she said smiling and looking pleased about something "I'm going to learn Spanish!" she said happily, with all the conviction of one who finds other languages easy "Thought he might appreciate the sounds of his mother tongue" Sue must have had an extra large language area inside her brain, she jumped into foreign languages, just like a cat jumps onto the table, and spoke French, German, and Russian like a native, whilst I struggled along with Spanish for beginners finding I never knew the necessary three or even two words.

I didn't hear the rest of what she said, because suddenly brakes squealed. At that moment David, our handsome young vet, swept down the track, and swerved into the yard. He was driving his beloved, superior to any land rover, Volvo as he came rallying round the corner. The Volvo proceeded to slither sideways over the ice covered cobbles, before spinning a tight circle and miraculously stopping a few centimeters from the barn wall.

"Cold up here Norma" David said tetchily, still shaking from his near collision, and buffeting by the icy cold wind.

"We keep on breathing David" I couldn't help but notice his blood red eyes, and pale grey skin color, he usually looked so healthy. The boys suffering from a serious lack of sleep I thought.

"Six hour vigil with a foaling mare last night" he said wearily and not one damn cup of tea for the worker. I'm frozen to the bone, and desperately tired" he moaned through chattering teeth.

"I'll make you a large mug of tea David" Sue's kind offer brought a wide grin to his exhausted appearance. Sue secretly adored David with his shock of golden curls and tall muscular frame.

"New horse, name of Ganador requires vaccinations and blood tests" he said reading the message in his diary.

"What a nice horse" he added, staring admiringly towards Ganador. "Different" he said appreciatively "A certain Grecian air about him, some fine breeding in this Lad, I'll be sure"

64

Ganador sang his reply, and then stood quietly as David skillfully stuck needles into his neck "Blood test results should be ready in three days." As David carefully labeled the phials to be sent away for testing, I outlined the stallions past injuries, or the ones that I knew of.

"Lengthy" he said grimacing on hearing the words stifle and back "sizably so."

"On the proviso he was given a full six month rest following his injuries, and there being no joint damage, careful training plus good nutrition can sometimes work wonders. But if he has any joint deterioration, I'm afraid you may be facing a losing battle Norma" David closed his large case, and grinned over his pint pot of sweet tea.

"You are so bloody negative David" remarked Geoff, who stood listening outside the loosebox door "I pay you to be positive"

"Can't be positive and honest Geoff, can I?" replied David. There was no skin off David's nose, Yorkshire men lived by a code of unwritten rules, the first being total freedom of expression, or the right to insult each other as and when they so wished.

"He could do with a bit more flesh on his bones though. Plenty of tea and scones Sue" said David walking out into the yard.

"But he has tea with milk and sugar every morning" said Sue gleefully, smiling at David's puzzled expression.

"Lovely horse, but I'm worried by the almost complete absence of muscle on his back" I heard David say to Geoff, in a quiet, private way.

"So am I David" replied Geoff abruptly "If we assume the worst, some kind of past breakdown or muscle damage, might there be a possibility for the muscle to rebuild?"

David rubbed his chin with his index finger, he always did this when the answer stumped him.

"David's automatic answer pilot just failed" whispered Sue, eagerly waiting for his reply.

"It all depends on the degree of atrophy involved, his overall soundness, and his age" he replied as though reading from a text book "Why not allow him to relax for a few weeks, before starting any retraining? But as for training Geoff- you know far more than I do about putting muscle onto his back, if that be possible of course"

Shortly after David rallied away, in his mud covered Volvo, the violent rain changed to thin light drizzle, and the flat slate colored sky seemed to fall even lower over the surrounding moors, bringing an eerie darkness that blotted out any remaining shafts of light. By 4, the gale force wind had become calm and still, with a feeling of imminent snow.

"It's so unfair" said Sue resentfully "My two days of shopping therapy have just been cancelled by this horrible moorland weather, and the forecast for Leeds is bright and sunny, according to Mum" she added heatedly, looking up at the low, heavily laden sky.

"Life's unfair Sue" replied Geoff in his best deadpan male way "You just have to put up with it."

After dinner, eaten in the north facing kitchen, Sue, Geoff, me and the dogs Ram, Dan and Scamp, relocated into the cozy sitting room, where we occupied the same positions each evening. The dogs squeezed into the only spaces left free on the hearth, between wood burning stove, and fireplace pillars whilst Sue sat in close proximity to the television, laughing along with her imaginary soap friends, skillfully knitting scarves and wooly gloves for Christmas presents, without once looking down.

The sofa was owned by Geoff, positioned in front of the stove, he would flake out in a collapsed horizontal position, with a comforting beer placed by his side. I sat in the only other warm spot, the rocking chair, and tried hard to read, but my thoughts kept on returning to Ganador, and the coming of spring, which was after all just around the corner.

How I longed for springtime. I closed my eyes imagining steaming mist clouds hovering like a sea over the thawing earth of the valley… When the clouds were nowhere to be seen and distant hilltops climbed into a perfect blue sky. I dreamed of climbing into bed without the addition of woolly socks and long johns… Walking between house and stables unmolested by freezing weather, but most of all I wanted to listen to the song of the blackbirds…and the call of the cuckoo each morning at dawn.

The sound of Geoff's voice swiftly disturbed my dreams "Norma" Geoff raised his eyebrows in an enquiring manner "Can you remember who… said that Spanish horses could be lethal in retraining?"

"Yes of course I remember. It was Manuel" I glanced at Geoff, wondering why his mind was on the dangers of retraining. Geoff knew the risks involved well, he often trained problem horses.

"But Ganador's here now, complete with past baggage" I could only guess at the degree of danger involved in the stallions retraining and for the first time in three eventful days I had a nagging doubt about 'running after my dream.'

"Mark rode him to the shop" Right away I realized what a stupid statement I'd made.

"Riding bareback to the shops, whilst smoking a fag cannot be compared to any training?" Geoff opened the fridge door to search out a beer "There are no short cuts in correct training" He slammed the fridge door as if to emphasize his words.

"Training is about obedience, developing the paces, building up the correct muscles. Training is about discipline, and that goes for both horse and rider." Geoff had an expression of controlled anger that warned me to keep quiet "And every time I look at Ganador, I'm fully aware that no muscle has ever been developed"

Of course I realized there were no short cuts in training. Correct training was a science, which consisted of discipline, total commitment, vast knowledge and harmony with the horse. The day to day aims when preparing a young horse were exactly the same as in ballet, perfection and suppleness of movement, impulsion, regularity of rhythm and poise. The end result should appear balanced, precise and relaxed yet still be exciting to watch.

Oh no, there were definitely no short cuts in dressage.

I will always remember the first time I met Manuel, and saw him ride. We were in Austria staying at the lovely home of a member of the Spanish Riding School… Hans was giving Geoff tuition in the riding of high school movements. Shortly before lunch on Thursday, Manuel and his wife Lourdes arrived from Portugal, and that same evening, Manuel gave a display of High School riding.

His display was both exciting and amazing. As I watched Manuel ride, I felt as if I'd found some treasures from the past. For I observed everything that I had always strived for, displayed in a style of riding, I did not even understand.

It was as though the horse, a black Lusitano stallion, performed everything as if free. There was great impulsion, supreme lightness, horse and rider performing the most difficult movements with precision and joy. From then on, we visited Portugal time and again, to watch Manuel ride and train.

It was Manuel who first introduced us to the world of Portuguese riding and classical master's. Through Manuel, I went on to meet the great masters of classical riding, Nuno Oliveira, Fernando D'Andrade, and watched training I had never believed possible. I owe so much to Manuel. I often thought of his words, and his brilliant horsemanship.

'Training is art, it is not force. Training takes much time, patience and knowledge, it cannot be hurried' Manuel would often reaffirm this fact 'Never rush in order to perform what is written on the test sheet, you will confuse and ruin your horse. Work always on achieving harmony with your horse, then perfect balance through the use of transitions, until the horse allows you to express your wishes through him'

'When training goes wrong, it is the fault of the rider. It is the riders who need correcting, not the horses' he would say spitting out every word. "I see many ruined Spanish horses. The Spanish horse must first be trained to move freely forwards in his basic paces. This is because the Spanish Horse has a talent for collecting himself together but not moving forwards... therefore any collected work must be 'put aside.' This is common sense, as you say... But there are riders, with little knowledge or sympathy for the horse, who wish to 'play to the crowd.' They want to show off the horse, by riding much piaffe and passage... without basic flat work. Sometimes the horse revolts, he is confused, and he refuses to move forwards. When this happens, riders with money, bring the horse to Portugal for retraining. By this time, the aptitude for collection can develop into rearing or jumping upwards, but not proceeding forwards. But alas, some horses can never be retrained, as they are broken down physically and scarred mentally. Some men think the horse is merely a machine'

Since Manuel's retirement, life had never been quite the same.

When I returned to the sitting room, Geoff sat at my desk, he looked up quickly. To my surprise he was leafing through Ganador's long impressive ancestry.

"I did say he looked impressive, the very first time I set eyes on him" Geoff grinned, raising his eyebrows, and for a moment I thought I saw the briefest trace of apology in his eyes. Suddenly I felt a pang of regret for heaping any dangers onto Geoff's shoulders.

"Don't worry" he said calmly "I'm perfectly happy about schooling your battle horse" Geoff smiled, and poured himself a beer.

Any further thoughts of dangers were quickly pushed aside, without the vaguest flicker of guilt. Inwardly I sighed with relief upon hearing Geoff's words.

"It's not worth getting stressed about, at least not yet. The next few weeks are taken care of, we all need a rest. Then we start slowly, very slowly; re-assess his condition regarding health and soundness. No point in thinking any further than that, now is there?"

Without further ado, Geoff reached for 'The Spanish Horse,' a fascinating book by Fernando D'Andrade which stood on the top shelf of the book case: and started to read.


*'Nothing is certain but the unforeseen'*
*Proverb.*

# 9. A Flying Start

*Toby Jug Farm March 16 1980*

I awoke to a world of startling white. Gleaming new snow blanketed the moors as it did every March, driving all living creatures to the lower parts of the valley where the river ran unfrozen and the rocky ledges offered some protection from the freezing winds. Even the crumbling stone walls lay buried and unseen under layers of new snow lending a neat Christmas card appearance to the surrounding countryside. Roads and pathways would remain hidden for many days to come, bringing a still, empty silence across the surrounding wilderness.

There were three more days of silence and brilliant light. On the fourth day a wind started to howl, and rain fell as ice, with hailstones the size of pebbles. Green grass appeared on the pasture after two weeks of rain and the marvel of early springtime came round once more.

*Diary*

'Very soon, the spring thaw will begin. Torrents of water from the moor will send a stream of muddy water down the farm track then over the pasture, before finding the river that runs through the gorge. The mud soaked arena will give Geoff the excuse he needs to start working Ganador in the school.

Four weeks have passed since the arrival of Ganador and inside these few weeks I feel I'm getting to know the stallion better. As his health improves he's losing that angular look. His neck doesn't look like a flag pole any more, neither can I see his ribs - and a big plus - his suspicion about those around him is definitely less. All in all I'm delighted with him – but its early days yet'

"He's ready for some slow work" said Geoff "Pointless putting it off any longer" Geoff was right, there was no point in delaying Ganador's training now the rains were here. I felt concerned that the moment he started proper work one of his past injuries might return and put him out of work for good "If he can't manage light work, he's no good for anything, remember what I said about starting slowly to re-assess his soundness? You have to think of what's best for the horse"

"But he may not be easy"

"Nothing's ever easy"

The following morning Geoff began the first phase of Ganador's work on the lunge, totally unprepared for what was to come, and how complex his problems would prove to be.

Geoff began by walking at his side, Ganador looked calm, even tranquil. He knew he had nothing to fear for Geoff walked round the school every day with him. We lengthened the side reins almost to the last hole, hoping he would stretch down and use his back. Geoff played the line out a little but still kept close to the stallion, close enough to remove any suspicion, and keep him moving forwards.

Without any warning Ganador stopped dead, lowering his quarters he went into a manic, relentless piaffe, the likes of which I had never seen before. The moment he stopped, I walked over to remove the side reins, with only one thought 'calm down Ganador, please.' Geoff walked over to rub the stallion's nose... he said

"I'm not forcing you boy – only requesting"

Once again Geoff encouraged him forwards, he said "trrrrrot on." As he moved forwards Ganador hesitated and then suddenly jumped into the air, he looked like a coiled spring landing in almost the exact spot he departed from. He then turned working trot into a series of caprioles, rears, and crazy panic. Before each sequence of leaps there was a brief pause, after which all hell was let loose. As suddenly as he started he stopped. He stood very tall, ears pricked and alert, listening for the slightest sound. For a long second he stood motionless. His black eyes so very wild, thinking only of his present danger. There was no longer any question as to why Ganador reacted in such a way. He'd obviously been hurt many times, challenged and provoked. Past experiences had taught him that men could be beaten, that he was the stronger and possessed far more strength – something a horse should never know. The stallion knew that men were not to be trusted, and at this point, I asked myself 'will he ever trust a man again?'

"I'm very patient" Geoff said more to himself than to Ganador "I can wait" When Ganador decided to walk calmly, Geoff encouraged him forwards for a second time. Once more he danced a rapid piaffe; abruptly he froze, before soaring into the air as though attempting to fly. Completing a circle, loop or square shape was not the problem. The difficulty Ganador had seemed to be in staying earth bound. Geoff changed the lunge line to a clip rope and started leading him round the school.

"Lesson over" he said "Have to start somewhere. Call it a learning curve from now on" But he must have seen my worried expression "Try to be positive. You are just wasting energy being negative. He'll learn" Had Geoff never noticed how my brain worked? How the words 'why' and 'what if' formed a barrier to even understanding the meaning of the word positive. The way Geoff thinks is as distant from me as Mars, and that's a long way.

Sue looked amazed. She'd been hard at work timing his lunge rounds on her diving watch. "Norma" she shouted excitedly "I've timed his rounds, and his longest single circle is timed at fifty two seconds. I think he's thrilling. Just imagine having the ability to perform all those airs above the ground" she said proudly "I think he's cool."

Thrilling or cool, I was desperately in need of advice. I needed help. If only Fernando was here and not in Portugal. Then I remembered how Fernando had insisted I contact him "whenever you need me." So I returned to the house, rang the international operator, and scribbled down questions I wanted to ask. Would he remember me? Was he still living in Estoril? On hearing Fernando's unmistakable voice my relief was immense, and I plunged right in, unloading all that I knew of Ganador's history and problems down the phone line, without remembering to say my name.

"It is Norma?" Fernando replied, in his impeccable English. "Unfortunately, I have seen horses like him, many times. Something in his early training has made him revolt. Your stallion has been made into a rebel who is capable of fighting man with his every breath; if he foresees training!"

"But will he ever trust a man again?"

"It will take a long time, and much patience" Fernando said in his usual unhurried way "But it may be possible, perhaps. Tell me, where did you find the horse?"

"He was with some travelling people...I fell in love with him"

"And you never watched him move?"

"The rain was torrential... I realize how stupid I was" Fernando sighed. I pictured him smiling.

"You were naïve perhaps... but then it's easy to fall in love with a horse...I know, it's happened to me. And Ganador sounds very intelligent, perhaps too intelligent. Tell me the names on his registration papers" at that moment I breathed a little easier, Fernando appeared interested, fascinated even.

As I rummaged through the drawers there was one thought in my mind 'please don't say Ganador's line is dangerous or even unreliable' I stumbled through the strange Spanish names on his Carta de Origen... Beautiful names, like Nevada, Destinada, Primeroso, Bilbaino and I read them slowly back to Fernando.

"Ah yes, I know of the line and there are not many about with his breeding," Fernando's impressed. I can hear it in his voice.

"What was he used for...riding, driving, stud?"

"He was used as" and I began to stammer "as a guard horse in a scrap yard"

"Ah... The horse was a guard horse; you mean he patrolled like a dog? I have no doubt he excelled in his work..."

"Better than any guard dog, or so I was told"

"But Ganador is far braver than a dog, and a great deal more valiant than any man Norma! Today horses are bought for sport, not battle or guarding!" Fernando sounds amused. I can just imagine him, smiling at my lack of common sense, his head in his hands "Horses like Ganador were bred for combat, and unfortunately he's never received any basic training… except in security. His evasions will be difficult problems to correct, especially with a full blooded stallion like Ganador… always assuming there are no physical problems of course.

You must always remember that Ganador carries the blood of fighting horses, from centuries before."

"What do you mean - I really can't imagine horses fighting?"

"But they did…Iberian horses and men were brought up to fight, and both showed amazing valor on the battlefield"

"Do you mean that Ganador might still retain the same fighting skills?"

"Exactly… It was the Iberian horse that gave to the Spanish forces their great superiority in battle, and Ganador is from one of the last remaining pure Spanish lines. Even today, horses of pure Iberian descent are ridden by our Caveleiro's to fight the brave torros in the bullrings of Portugal. Chosen because of their high intelligence, bravery and lightning reactions" Fernando spoke so very proudly. "It is possible, that when Ganador was young, he refused to accept the bullying methods handed out to lesser horses. His line is much too arrogant to put up with fools or bullies - therefore, he's gradually come down the ladder, until you found him in a scrap yard. Most men are afraid of stallions such as Ganador, because he's too clever and there are very few trainers with sufficient ability to even consider the retraining of such a mixed up horse. But tell me more about him"

"He appears to want to fly – to soar through the air. I know it sounds stupid"

"Oh no, you are seeing his leaping abilities. Some historians think the old line may once have been behind the legend of the Centaurs. This is because they possess more ability in moving upwards than in moving forwards - And this is the source of his problems, he has never been sent forwards." he told me, "Thus he uses his natural ability in leaping to fight you, exactly as he fought his first trainer, when undoubtedly he won" he said with conviction "I have seen this happen, believe me....... To this day his line is used when introducing height and vigor into airs above the ground - it is used by the Spanish Riding School of Vienna – it is used to breed the bravest bull fighting horses" There was a hint of excitement in Fernando's voice "Horses such as Ganador changed the course of history"

"But Fernando," I said desperately "I am not intending to fight in the bull rings of Portugal or Spain. Neither do I want to fly through the air..." The moment I replied, I realized my words were perhaps rather tactless "Please tell me what I should do?" I pleaded "I know of the Lusitano stallion you retrained after every other training yard refused to take him in, I saw the horse in Lisbon, and he looked awesome." I hoped this observation would please him.

"Obrigado Norma. You are very observant!" Thank goodness he sounded pleased once more. For a few moments' he became silent. I imagined him running his fingers through his hair, the way he always did when thinking hard.

"There is a way... a very slow tedious method" His words seemed to hang in the air "A way which might help, depending on the extent of atrophy in the muscle. You must lunge him for short periods with his head down. During the first week of lunging you will need the balancing rein but only for the first three minutes. After three minutes, change to long side reins"

"So it may be possible...?"

"I think it may well be possible, if you follow these rules. You must never tire him... I cannot over emphasize the importance of timing training minutes carefully – we are strengthening not weakening. The second rule is to think of him as a child who has to do physiotherapy exercises to become stronger and more flexible... But the third rule is perhaps the most important, it is to repeat the basics over and over again all through training. Maybe after six weeks he will find ten minutes possible? But then it all depends on the extent of physical damage, and the level of weakness involved"

I sensed Fernando raising his eyebrows as he scribbled down a training plan "Do not include canter, he is not yet strong enough, and endeavor to maintain a slow relaxed trot. If he finds walk to trot transitions difficult, walk closer to him. This will be a good workout for you too, yes? Do not back off and never show anger" Suddenly he went quiet, our conversation over, at least for now. So I thanked him, promised to obey his instructions and to contact him regularly with progress reports "Norma, I will tell you everything I know. Chow!" and with these comforting words Fernando's voice had gone.

I delayed the introduction of this piece of equipment for a few more days, hoping a miracle might happen and he would suddenly become normal and forward going. After all flying horses did not exist. Flying horses existed in legend and myth, not in fact… Or did they? Horses covered the ground horizontally, in the paces of walk, trot, and canter. Leaping into the air was not in their vocabulary, or was it? So I researched the legends surrounding the Spanish horse. One of the legends described a herd of Spanish horses as being like 'sons of the wind,' horses that could almost fly. They lived in the hills and valleys of south western Iberia and were believed to possess amazing speed and leaping ability, a gift that allowed them to soar into the air from valley to hill. By far the most beautiful legend suggested that ancient Iberian horses provided the inspiration behind the 'Centaurs,' man horse creatures said to spring into the air from the valleys. Even stranger legends praised the early Iberian war horse, fabled by some to have been a supernatural creature, wild and uncontrollable. Maybe Ganador had inherited a few of these odd characteristics? After all there's no smoke without fire, legend or no legend…

Following several extra days of achieving nothing but panic or airs above the ground we all agreed there was no alternative but to obey Fernando's advice; exactly in the manner he had ordered. Geoff dusted down the old lunging bridle, he renewed the mouse eaten cord with new, and he puzzled over what went where. Sue cleaned and softened the rock hard leather, polishing the buckles until they shone.

"Whatever is this thing?" Sue remarked "And how do you remember where to fix the cord?" she said continuing to polish the shining brass buckles.

"It's a training aid Sue; personally I don't like them, "but Fernando insists – he says it will help to develop Ganador's back muscles"

"What does Geoff think?"

"He agrees…"

"But why use it? If a horse likes to keep his head high, so what? Sue grimaced as she hung the leather reins up with the tack "If horses were in need of this 'thing' they would have been born with it already on."

"This 'thing' compels a horse to use his back, lower his head and engage the hind legs. Hopefully the end result is relocating muscle on the top line. Think of it as a body building device!" I soothingly replied "We must think of him as a child who has to do physiotherapy exercises in order to be stronger…"

Still not happy, she examined the tack again, "Anything to do with body building is torture to me" Sue was always truthful, and she did have a point. I also hated equipment, but somehow we had to put muscle onto that poor, wasted back. If we failed he would never move forwards with ease and balance. 'A well muscled and supple back can add up to ten years to the working life of the horse' Fernando had once said 'The long working lives of the Lipizzaner prove this.' But then Ganador wasn't a young Lipizzaner?

Ganador showed his disgust concerning the new routine by refraining from calling out in his usual melodious whinnies. He was silent, totally so towards Geoff his trainer, replacing his usual welcoming calls with hard bruising nips, whenever he caught sight of the device.

"Ganador has more sense than most of the human race put together"

"That's not saying much is it"

"Ganador agrees with me, he also thinks it looks like torture equipment, what a sensible horse he is" Ganador handed out a more than playful nip to Geoff, whilst he prepared him for lungeing, as if agreeing with Sue.

Following six weeks of lungeing in the 'a la Fernando' style, plus enormous quantities of food, we were all thrilled to see that some improvement had been made. The sharp bony ridge of vertebrae appeared less prominent, his back began to feel a little softer, and the earliest beginnings of muscle development could be seen to be forming. This was an enormous breakthrough, and exactly what we had been waiting for, a definite step in the right direction.

*

That night I rang Fernando, with my report of the past six weeks training. After the usual formal niceties of chat, I found it impossible to stay quiet any longer "Ganador's looking much better. There's getting to be some muscle on his back, I can see it! And he's moving forwards for a full ten minutes. I think we may be turning our first corner. Do we continue with the work... Is it more of the same?" Why did I ask? For I already knew the reply.

"The short answer is 'yes.' Every day you must persist. Each week add one minute more... If he finds it difficult repeat the basics. You know we are not asking much?" he said gently "In the next lessons we must endeavor to attain fifteen minutes of forward relaxed movement, this is the maximum time of use. Then use the long side reins with walk - trot transitions."

"But how can we help his panic attacks?"

"We can't. The panic he shows is that of self defense. This will never completely depart, however it will slowly become less: I promise you it will. On one condition, that he is never placed under too much stress" Fernando always helped me to see the real problem, the one that lay hidden under the surface.

"These difficulties are not for the faint of heart... You will need skill, persistence and much knowledge. A trainer must learn to be satisfied with little or no steps forward, and when to ask for that bit more. It pays to be sympathetic when a horse finds his work difficult, meet him half way, and never lose his calm. Without calm there can be no training. Later, when he is strong enough to ride, we will ask more, and then you will require bravery too… but he is not yet prepared for the second part of his training" Fernando had seen all these difficulties many times before.

"You must learn to accept him, and be proud of his ways. For your stallion is not a normal horse, he is a very special horse. His ancestors were leaders of armies, who carried Kings into battle. Ganador's breed became the model for the whole of Europe 'the horse of courtly splendor' and no royal court could buy Spanish lines in sufficient numbers. He was sought after, unrivalled, both as a battle horse and a parade horse and later as a dressage horse. He created the art of equitation… Classical riding and the Spanish horse cannot be separated, and the art of dressage at its most advanced level was developed in order to copy the unique natural abilities of the Spanish horse. Natural abilities that fashioned a new art form"

"But how does an art form begin to develop, to be used for pleasure?"

"It must be available at the right time in history, seen in the right place, with people who take pleasure in the new art"

"There are so many obstacles in the way"

"But obstacles are put there to be cleared! I think it first began to grow after the Romans took Sevilla. They named the city Bastika, and built an amphitheater that could seat many thousands of spectators. Nowhere was there such enjoyment and pleasure of spectacle than with the Romans – a civilization that admired the movements of the Spanish Horse and worshipped his bravery. Perhaps it was at this point the first seeds of the new art were sown"

"Who sowed the next seeds?"

"Over three hundred years later, Spain was invaded by the Moors, who brought with them a great love of the horse. The Arabs created a picture of the Spanish horse that travelled through the World and developed hundreds of descriptive terms for the horse… Lots of them highly poetical. So you can see how the foundations developed - how it strengthened and grew into a new art form that was rich with possibilities, that later took Europe by storm. Riders throughout Europe wanted to copy the natural abilities of the Spanish Horse on their non Spanish horses, heavier and less active breeds. Every rider wanted to reproduce his collected and elevated steps. And this was only the beginning"

"When did riding masters emerge?"

"The new art of classical riding became introduced into Italy at the turn of the fifteenth century, when the Spanish cavalry defeated the French gendarmerie in a rather undignified and all too easy manner, and then pushed forwards in all haste towards Naples. And it is here that we find the very first riding academies, which were later to spread throughout the whole of Europe. The new art of horsemanship and the training of horses was to become a very important part in the life of every man during the middle ages! This new art, called for the invention of methods of training, which in turn gave rise to Riding Academies, teachers, treatises, which in turn required the development of new fangled often cruel methods of training. Most of the earlier trainers followed the methods of the Romans. Although the Romans admired the Spanish horse, they did not understand that he must be a willing partner, and not a fearful slave. Horses broke down quickly, because they were not strong enough, not able to carry out the movements asked for. Only the Spanish horse had the morphology to perform the airs of high school, without any special preparation. Sadly the earlier trainers believed any breed of horse could endure the roughness of repeated exercises. And like the Romans had no appreciation of the long hours necessary in training a horse to obey willingly. So they turned to force, using harsh lever bits, savage spurs and lashing whips to get their results... All this suffering to copy the natural movements of the Spanish horse. And sadly some of these methods are in use even today."

"But why is the Spanish horse hardly ever seen when he's played such an important part in our history?"

"It is all because the Spanish horse does not fit the requirements of today's sports! But it is certainly not for the Spanish horse to worry about such mundane things. No, the classically bred Iberian horse must remain untarnished - which is only possible if there are

**Ganador V 1981. Horse of Kings and Emperors',
brave, fearless and incredibly noble.**

**Head Study**

**Morning drive Sevilla, Ganador right**

**Grand Master Nuno Oliveira (sketch)**

**Ganador in tranquil mood, Geoff riding**

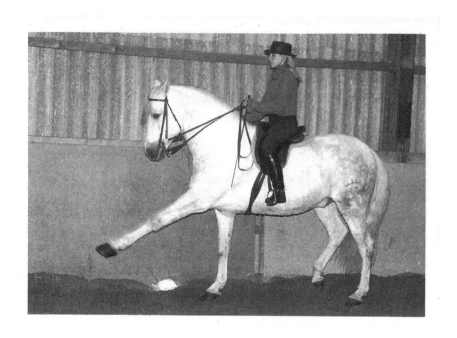

**Ganador, Pas Espagnol**

'Look no hands' Maestro Manuel Sabino Duarte

**Training in Vienna, author riding**

sufficient breeders who wish to conserve his unique qualities..."

"I never knew that horses like Ganador helped form our culture - make our civilization what it is today"

"Throughout history the role of the Spanish horse has molded European civilization. Did you know the Capriole jump was used in battle to kill foot soldiers, long before the sixteenth century? The pure Iberian horse is the result of careful breeding from the finest lines over centuries, breeding for his beauty, his bravery, and abilities in combat. He was the envy of the world, faithfully guarding his master, and at all times prepared to fight to his death.

This is verified by ancient Iberian art works which clearly show the equestrian combat horse savaging and striking his unfortunate victims. Dogs also were used, to bite and savage the heels of enemy warriors, the dogs being protected from flying arrows by suits of armor.

There is much evidence to show that the early Iberian horse fought, as did his master, and both horse and rider showed amazing valor and bravery on the battle field. What your stallion possesses is inherited from his forefathers. He is a work of art, a living breathing work of art" I felt stunned by Fernando's words. "His past owners have not appreciated his history or his requirements." Fernando spoke kindly but firmly.

"Horses such as 'Ganador' are our heritage" he paused, and his voice softened "And so we cannot punish him for his birthright, can we?" Fernando sighed deeply "In the past he's been treated unfairly, learned to use his fighting abilities. He would most possibly have been shot, if you had not rescued him. His experiences with men have taught the stallion a dangerous lesson... that a man can be beaten. In 'his' mind he has conquered every man, and men do not like to look fools!" Fernando's voice held a trace of sadness, no doubt he had often witnessed brutality from his fellow man, towards horses with problems.

"He's been well and truly messed up" My heart dropped as I spoke these words "Geoff always says violent trainers are incompetent"

"What a horse does under compulsion, he does without

understanding. Geoff is correct- you have to learn patience, and acceptance of the stallion's mental and physical condition? I suggest there is a great deal of consistency in his daily work, so he is familiar with his routine, and then his surprises may become fewer!"

"With a little luck, and if at all times you follow my instructions; he will at some point decide to work with you. He will come to trust you, because he knows you will never ask more of him, than he is able to give" he sighed "But remember it will be sometimes, and not always that he will trust you and work with you. Nonetheless, once we have a little of his trust… he will never again be 'always' against you!" he made these words ring with the conviction that only a Master Trainer would dare to prophesy.

"Muito obrigado Fernando" I replied, knowing that it was never possible to thank someone with such vast expertise, who was at all times prepared to pass on his knowledge.

"The main rule for good work is to maintain the calm of the horse- at every stage of training. First of all, we re-establish tranquility . . ." Fernando's voice had disappeared.

Of course he was correct. Ganador would take every last ounce of our patience. Fernando had retrained many highly temperamental stallions after their less skillful owners had given up on them. Just to watch his technique and listen to his guidance told me his advice was sound in approach, often inspiring. From our first meeting I think he willingly accepted he was now my mentor. There was nothing said to that effect, but I felt no surprise when his first letter arrived only weeks later.

*'On its brow it carries the brilliant mark of the morning'*
*Al Andaluz 1295.*

# 10. City of the Sea

*Toby Jug Farm April 20, 1980.*

There were six saddles in the tack room, all sat neatly on shiny red racks… and all waited to be cleaned. Stepping on a mounting block I carefully lifted the first saddle down. It was Portuguese, a Sela Ribatejo. The one Geoff had fallen in love with when in Lisbon.

'This saddle is far more comfortable than most armchairs' he'd said, with a look of longing in his eyes 'But it's too expensive' So the dealer slashed his price and we bought it, only to find the width was too narrow for any horse in our yard. A detail that didn't seem to matter, for by then the saddle had become like a good friend, we loved having it around. As I cleaned its high Baroque style cantle, I remembered touching the saddle for the very first time. The city was Lisbon Portugal; the time springtime and the year nineteen seventy six.

When we clear the airport Geoff wants to take a tram "Let's walk to where the trams stand" On the road outside there's a tank, it's parked as though guarding the entry. The gun turret's positioned so as to point menacingly towards the road.

"I can imagine it following me, even though I know its still. Wish we'd taken a taxi"

"Don't be silly" he replied "probably a hunting party. Remember what Dad said and don't get carried away" At the tanks side are a group of men, unshaven and wearing camouflage, they look deep in conversation, and all carry guns with full shoulder slung bandoliers. I try not to stare, but find it difficult. My eyes seem to be glued to them.

The day before I flew out I'd rung Dad, partly to satisfy Geoff, he kept going on about the hazards of flying in war zones.

"Is Lisbon safe Dad?"

"There's no problem" he told me "Just one or two rebels hanging about, but nothing to be concerned about." I always contacted Dad before boarding any flight; he knew what was going on in the world.

"But Geoff thinks there's a problem?"

"There is a problem, but it's not a war" Dad had said "Just redistribution of power, to the left wing. Just keep your head down and remember the rules. You can dance down the street with a leftist, but land owners and the wealthy are being watched, particularly in the Alentejo district"

"But why are they watched?"

"Land around a city is always valuable. The left wing is probably eyeing it up. In other words, they want the land" I didn't understand politics, never had, but this didn't sound like politics, at least not the sort I knew.

"Eyeing the owners up too?"

"Let's just say that I wouldn't want to own land in that region…"

"There" I said to Geoff "Just politics, nothing to worry about"

He shrugged. His face seemed worried, but he knew he'd lost the argument, so he went ahead and told me what he thought.

"Well I think that handing out A.K's to peasants is dangerous, and so does Dad, but he can't stop you going… and neither can I"

"Why don't you come along Geoff?" And to my surprise Geoff agreed.

"Book two seats then" he said "May as well make the most of a quiet time" So I went ahead and booked another seat. This could be the last chance I'd ever get to watch a show given by Fernando and his trainers…

Maybe Geoff was correct, and the men outside the airport were members of a hunting party standing next to an abandoned tank? But what is there to hunt between concrete and the Ocean? May as well forget them, whatever they were up to is bloodless, everyone looks to be getting on with their lives… And surely this is the most important thing, a society without chaos. Or is it? Only the wealthy and owners of land seem to have suffered  - fascists as they are called… Workers are acceptable, but now there's no work, sweeping strikes have seen to that. The army seems to have looked after the peasants - armed them with Kalashnikovs, given them orders to occupy land even. It has to be a purge on the wealthy. Thank goodness the trouble only appears to be around Lisbon. I say appears- but without living there I can only guess.

I quickly forget about the men and the tank when we board a tram leaving for Campo Grande. At our destination we walk through a park. The sky shines a brilliant blue, and the sun feels warm, hot even. I start to relax, enjoy myself, this is paradise compared to the freezing cold of the moors. All around me I breathe in the magical scent of the sea… Strong and salty, the freshness of the Ocean. I remember Fernando saying Lisbon is the sea. He calls it the city of the sea. Blue Jacaranda trees blossom in the parks and the haunting strains of Fado music echoes softly from open windows.

"Whatever are you crying for?" I try to turn away but too late, Geoff's seen my tears.

"It's always the same when I hear mournful melodies" I sobbed "makes me feel sad" I undergo an emotion that stops me in my tracks, my feet refuse to walk, tears run down my cheeks "I want to stop and listen in" I say hopelessly.

"Let's stop right here" So we sit outside a café listening to the haunting melodies of Fado until the sad mood passes

"Lisbon in spring is magic"

"Certainly different to Yorkshire" And we walk down the street laughing.

Lisbon, the old city of Olissipo is like a fairy tale, it's a place steeped in myth and legend, where the shores of the Atlantic Ocean meet the mouth of the river Tagus, 'where there once lived a herd of horses who could almost fly'. The home of 'la Cavalo Lusitano' once considered the best saddle horse in the world.

On rounding a corner we almost walk into a display of antique saddles spilling out across the pavement. Some were Persian, the rest Baroque Portuguese. All were classical in design, the more expensive embossed with silver and jewels. The saddles sparkle in the sunlight, as if showing the magnificence that characterizes the breed they were made for.

Inside the shop were less ornate saddles, still impressive but in a quieter way "Just look at this beauty it's a Sela Ribatejo"

"Manuels favorite saddle" And the rest was history.


After a rest on the waterfront we take a train up to the hills above Lisbon. Suddenly the crowded rooftops of suburbia give way to greenery and Roman ruins. Amid luxurious gardens, it's to be Manfred's final display and though four years have passed I remember every moment of that night as if it were yesterday.

"Who's giving the display?" asked Geoff.

"Manfred" I answer "He's one of Fernandos pupils"

"You know him then?"

"We met at Fernandos"

"Why is he leaving?"

"He's returning to his homeland"

"What a combination to take back home- Portuguese equestrian skill on the back of German discipline!"

Before the display, Fernando invites questions from the audience. Nothing is ever too much trouble for Fernando. For a few seconds, there's total silence. Perhaps no one can think of a question. So I slowly raise my hand, someone has to start things moving.

"How many years of preparation are required when training a horse to the level of High School?" Fernando searched for the hand, he recognized my voice and then he smiled. At that moment I felt pleased I'd made the effort to attend, it would have been so easy not to have bothered.

"There can be no time limit - my only wish is to work towards perfection. Haute ecole is an art. The airs of higher work are the final touches on the canvas. But, it is also an art that is capable of breaking down, before the ultimate brush stroke! Always I am ready to take the horse back to the basic principles." Fernando shrugged his shoulders "My rules are simple, preserve the calmness of the horse, and then ride forwards into straightness. Only then can he collect himself a little, as the rider desires. But to answer the question briefly, when the horse is between five to six years, or sufficiently mature I begin. I expect the training to 'take' between four to six years, on some occasions never. There is no time limit!"

For some reason, I cannot conjure up any intelligent reply. I never expected such a philosophical analysis.

He moved on to the next raised hand, probably a question from some expert who felt secure enough in his own knowledge to ask about the training of high school airs. When I saw it was Geoff's hand I felt dizzy with surprise. 'What are you asking?' I hissed. But Geoff wasn't listening.

"Do you train piaffe from the ground, or the saddle?"

The quiet tone of his voice seems to fill the airwaves. Fernando considered the question carefully, he smiled running his fingers through his hair, the way he always did when taken by surprise.

"You know, not many horses like to perform Piaffe; for a horse it is the most difficult movement, but to answer your question - I work on Piaffe from the ground and also in the saddle"

"But how does one train height and suspension?"

I was sure I saw a hint of a smile cross his face, as though he considered the question amusing.

"The height and elevation within any movement are the result of the rhythmic spring from behind, as well as the degree of collection. Only the strongest horses can ever achieve this. The majority of horses never develop sufficient strength and suppleness. Others do; but prefer never to be fully obliging!  I have to be aware of the capabilities of the horse when training this movement. My rule is to be content with little. Everything can be good when done with intelligence, but can be dangerous if not done well." Geoff doesn't speak. What can he say? There's something final about the words of Fernando. His answers appear impossible to contradict. He has that rare quality of assessing and establishing beyond any doubt, a clear understanding of the facts behind any problem. Some call the quality genius. I see him as a brilliantly gifted man, passionate in promoting the Iberian horse and its culture, through his writing, training and teaching.

As twilight is closing in, we see a magical display of equestrian art. I see the inner power of the man connecting with the mystical power of the Lusitano. The music's by Verdi its dramatic opera. A perfect choice to suite the mood he wants to create, on this his final performance. At exactly the right moment, colorful spotlights come to rest on the figures of horse and trainer - they stand motionless between the Romanesque pillars of a high arched entryway. Manfred is long reining, Fernando sometimes walking by his side

In the program I read about the horse and its breeding. It says the horse is a nine year old Lusitano entire, from the Andrade line. He's a superbly powerful animal; his color is bay, a brilliant shining bay. His long black mane and tail hang loose and unplaited. The horse is fully mature and strongly muscled displaying the best characteristics of the pure Iberian horse, nobility, glamour and a quick intelligence. Manfred walks close to the stallion's quarters in the Viennese style of long reining. A method that shows the horse is already highly schooled under saddle. The bay horse floats effortlessly into half pass right then left. In piaffe, the rhythmic spring is perfect; the passage hovering and elevated, his movements give the impression of controlled power. Directly out of piaffe the horse performs a transition into Spanish trot. His steps are high, brilliant and ground covering. I've never seen anything to match such equestrian perfection. The audience looks on intently, most of the ladies having already fallen under the influence of the men's skill.

Suddenly, the music changes, now he shows canter work, to the waltzes of Joanne Strauss. The stallion carries himself in perfect balance; he finds no difficulty when making rhythmically perfect sequence changes. When Fernando takes over, he shows the collected movements of ancient canter, canter in place, and canter to the rear. Movements, I've only read about in old riding manuals, always through a haze of disbelief. 16 C combat maneuvers, once necessary in battle, now only seen displayed in the bull rings of Portugal. Unexpectedly the bay leaps high into the air, and kicks back. He displays the Capriole jump… once used in battle to injure foot soldiers. The music ends, and then he halts, standing motionless, once more reminiscent of a statue. His brilliant bay coat damp with sweat, his long mane tangled and untidy, but no- one seems to care, if anything his wild appearance only adds to his magnificence.

Afterwards, we went out with Fernando's party of friends and riders. He chose a small café on the beach, close to the mouth of the Tagus.

"Let's sit on the beach first" I pleaded "Its magic" We sat on abandoned deckchairs surrounded by fishing boats and listened to the music of the sea. Foam from the sea spray sparkled silver under the light of the moon and the air was soft with its scent. Nothing seemed real that night. I think the feelings called drinking in the spirit of the moment… a magical moment.

After the meal we talked well into the night. No one mentioned Manfred's final display that was history now. Fernando spoke of devoting more time to his ranch, his treasure house of Iberian horses, all from the purest lines, the end product of a great deal of dedication and knowledge, founded by Dr Ruy D'Andrade, Fernandos late father and his father before him.

"Today, bull fighting is keeping the Iberian horse alive" Fernando said unexpectedly "And breeding good horses is not an easy science"

I delayed my question for as long as possible, I didn't want to offend Fernando, or any of his friends, not tonight. But the wine must have loosened my tongue. So ignoring the stares and Geoff's warning glance I went ahead with my question.

"Tell me Fernando; why is it that all Portuguese horse breeders are so totally engrossed in the breeding of bull fighting horses?" I tried to pass my question off as a joke, for I'd said what I didn't mean to say. There was silence for a time, and then Fernando smiled at my appalling lack of knowledge.

"You must realize Norma, that bull fighting here in Portugal, is the modern day equivalent of combat equitation, exactly as it was in Roman times?"

Of course I realized what Fernando in his tactful charming way was endeavoring to say, but I also remembered submitting a series of articles about the Portuguese style of riding, which included the words 'bull fighting,' I also remembered the day Sophie the editor fired one of her warning shots down the phone line "Too dangerous for the magazine, and for me - Anyway readers wouldn't like it.......All references to this strange pastime of bull fighting have to be written out. Please Norma?"

"But I thought readers wanted knowledge..."

"Not everyone does." Sophie was always bad mannered, so like a coward I agreed.

But even I could not understand the bigger picture, the passion shown in this corner of Portugal towards the breeding of bulls and horses.

"A good fighting horse is superior in every way to any other horse you care to mention" Fernando banged the table with his fist and for a moment the café became quiet.

"But why is he superior Fernando?" Geoff asked in an abnormally quiet voice "Disregarding his past of course"

"For instance, we need maneuverability in the smallest possible space, lightning reflexes, dancing steps, flexibility and strength... plus a high intelligence. Surely that is everything a rider could wish for in any equestrian discipline? One day the pendulum will swing back, and as it swings the pure Iberian horse will once again rise to fame. Until then he must be carefully preserved, so that his qualities remain the same. Portugal must never lose its remaining pure lines. And as the bulls become quicker, we cross the pure bred with the Arab- but always we keep the qualities of the pure bred"

"But todays competition riders want German horses" said Geoff "Big power packed warm bloods"

"Of course they do, German horses win!" Fernando smiled. As an International dressage judge he knew exactly which horse's riders were buying "He wins because he displays ground covering paces and good extensions... But too much emphasis is placed on extensions. Fashions change – they always do, always have, but traditions tend to linger. And the Iberian horse is part of a tradition that must never be allowed to die."

At that moment... I began to understand the obsession and unmistakable passion felt for the Iberian horse, so evident in this south western corner of Portugal where the river Tagus meets the Atlantic Ocean – Perhaps it's all about retaining Iberia's magnificent past, the fighting horses of Ancient times... That other world of long ago when men and horses were brought up to fight. And I thought of a story Mum used to tell me...

'Legend tells us that long, long ago there lived a race of people whose territory lay between the mouth of the Tagus and the Ocean Atlantic shores. They lived in the province of Lusitania, near the old city of Olissipo. The horses bred in this region were amazing for their speed and bravery; some say they were bred by the wind... One does not see the wind, and the marvel of the wind can perform many wonders'

"Norma, where are you?" Sue called insistently. I brought myself back to earth with a thud, dropping the saddle I was cleaning.

"Cleaning tack"

"Not making it?"

"Coming Sue" I knew my dreaming was over at least for now.

"Ganador's in the school, thought you wanted to watch him?"

"I do..." And I quickly positioned myself in the gallery, alongside Geoff. I loved watching the stallions thirty minutes of freedom, when the lack of any restrictions allowed him the chance to play. Perhaps he remembered his times of spending twenty three and three quarter hours a day standing in a stall, his freedom taken away. For in many parts of Europe young horses stand in stalls or minutely sized boxes, with only sufficient room to lie down.

"Just watch this Norma" shouted Sue as she kicked a football towards Ganador. The stallion wavered from left to right then amazingly headed the ball back with the side of his nose.

"Just call us G. F. C. or- Ganador's football club, we could apply for a stock market listing, be rich overnight"

In the meantime Ganador's fame was spreading; people had started to come from near and far to watch his daily exercise. His effect on the small farming community of Moonraker Heights had been startling. The locals were curious about Ganador. Moorland inhabitants had never seen such a horse, except in fairy books. Besides having glamour – he also had acting ability, and loved to show off. He was a novelty, he promised glimpses of an exciting world across the sea, with unheard of terrains. Ganador turned our stable yard into some kind of Promised Land where everyone wanted to be. Neighboring farmers excitedly watched his every move, even talked about him in the Pub. Ganador was newsworthy and he seemed to know it. He played to his daily audience with skill and expertise, accepting everyone's admiration without a second glance. Ganador never needed patting…for he knew he was a King. People quickly became captivated by his presence, sometimes even spellbound, in exactly the same way as I was…. Ganador allowed me to glimpse history, those wild, fighting horses of ancient times. He possessed a spirit that once had been widespread but could never be recreated in today's world. Maybe the people who were fascinated by him could also feel something extraordinary. After all, everyone needs to recapture history…

*'And the clouds cannot catch it*
*No matter how fast they fly,'*
*Al Andaluz 1295.*

# 11. Sue's Bombshell

*April 27.*

A few days later, Sue stopped watching her nightly fix of television soaps, I knew immediately something was wrong; she never missed her 'specials', she had what's called an addiction…

"I'm studying Spanish Norma" she kept saying "Far more interesting than television." But my suspicions had been aroused, I found it increasingly difficult not to observe her enthusiasm towards everything Spanish, possibly due to the growing number of text books, verb files, and dictionaries which started appearing just about everywhere in the house. Even the bathroom was not sacrosanct. Close to the toilet I'd placed a music stand, on which stood not my orchestral scores, but Spanish text books. Today's chapter heading read "Como te llamas?" On the shelf above the sink was a further book, shouting out words like "Saludar y desperdirse." But all was to become clear the following Monday morning.

"Norma" she spoke hesitantly, as if waiting for courage to arrive "I've been thinking- thinking hard about my life" I heard Sue's unspoken words before they were uttered -

"What's on your mind?" And then came the bombshell, the one I knew was about to fall… If I was honest.

"I want to see the world, live in different places - I don't want to feel trapped"

"What are you intending to do, or should I say – where are you planning to go?"

"Spain" she said without a moment's hesitation "I'd like to work

101

with horses in Southern Spain" So there it was, the obvious, the desire to travel, to move on. I suppose I'll just have to accept she's going.

Mum told me that nothing lasts forever. 'Welcome everything given willingly' she always said 'because it always ends sooner or later.'

I guess she's right. Still, losing Sue is hard to take. She's been a gem, a perfect groom, and that's saying something.

For some unclear reason, I'd put any thoughts of Sue leaving to the back of my mind. She's been with me two years, and life without her seems difficult to imagine.

"So you want to leave the Yorkshire moors... And work in Spain. That's a big jump" I try my hardest to sound lighthearted, but my voice doesn't obey "Have you a city in mind?"

"I think it's to be Seville!"

"The city of enchantment" What am I saying? I should tell her it's a horrible place, anything to make her change her mind, put her off going. But what I say doesn't matter now. She's made up her mind. End of story "I thought you were learning Spanish for the benefit of Ganador... He is bilingual" as I said his name, I immediately feel uneasy. It's not going to be a simple matter getting a groom. Not with Ganador about. And worry regarding the stallion, takes over my brain waves at the speed of light.

"Can you help me find a job out there?" Sue asked pleadingly. "That is of course, when we find someone else" What can I say? I feel trapped. Replacing her could be an impossible job. Anyone who has ever required the help of a good groom will have found that ninety per cent, call for constant supervision. And that makes the remaining ten per cent difficult to find "I've been thinking about Ganador, I mean his future care. Not many grooms will be capable of handling him. So I've devised a test for the applicants" She waits for my reply, and then looks at me to see if there's any feedback "Nervous people make him uneasy and we can't have that." Why does she sound so caring when she's about to abandon him? I pour one last coffee. A wave of stress is taking over as I imagine how Ganador might react to any show of incompetence. And then there's the little problem of Geoff…

After a few moments she adds one further problem.

"He hates people who try to bully him. You must be familiar with the dominant types? He can't stand any rough treatment"

"Don't worry Sue" Why did I keep saying 'don't worry' when all the worry's heaped on my shoulders? It's Sue who should be worrying, not me. She wants to be free to enjoy the World, not trapped on the moors like I am "Don't worry" There… I've said it again "Ganador refuses to allow certain people near him" I thought of Adams and the ones who went before "Most probably he would attempt to kill them"

"What time are you flying tomorrow?" There's something different in her tone of voice, something that I'd never heard before, a dreamy quality, wistful even. May as well accept it, Ganador has cast his magic spell on Sue, waved his wand over her. But where would I find another Sue? And what would Geoff say?

"Don't tell Geoff Sue. He's going to find out soon enough" And then I remembered, that Sue has every right to be free. The fact that I'm unhappy about losing her doesn't matter. It's her life and it's probably the best idea she's ever had.

"Promise not to tell, but please ask Maria if there might be a job for me out there? You are meeting Maria?"

"Meeting her tomorrow" Why do I feel so angry… it could be all hot air and dreams. I can't own a person for life- that's slavery. Sue's free and mobile, better get that clear.

"Where did you first meet Maria?" persisted Sue "She seems to hold the world in her hands regarding horses"

"If anyone can help you find a job… Maria can. Just don't say one word about this to Geoff"

"Promise not to tell" So I gave in to Sue's request and told her the tale of how I met Maria.

'Some years ago, Dad took me on holiday to Northern Portugal, it was a golfing break and Mum didn't want to go. So Dad and I went alone. The hotel was set on a peninsular, an away from it all place overlooking the sea. Not just to the front but all around. The sound was of Atlantic breakers crashing against cliffs, it hypnotized me with its never ending rhythm. For one full week, I left the balcony windows wide open, filling the room with the music of the sea"

"Did you meet her there?" Not to be hurried I carried on with my story.

'There were lifts down to the beach; it was a deep sheltered bay with fine white sand where rows of tiny striped tents stood side by side like soldiers. A young woman sat reading outside the neighboring tent to mine. She said her name was Maria.

"Have you come up North for the riding?" she asked.

"I didn't know there was any riding"

"It's the best riding country in Portugal" she said "And with fine Lusitano horses. Why not let me show you the countryside?"

From that first day we rode out every afternoon. We rode through pine forests spilling downwards to the sea on winding paths that led to secluded coves where we galloped in the shallows. And in the evening Maria joined us at dinner, after which we sat and talked.

I have never forgotten the stories she told me about the harassment she was getting from the police during the period of land reform.

Maria lived in the Alentejo area of Portugal close to Lisbon, where she and partner Enrique owned a small Coudelaria or horse breeding ranch, they were land owners. Some of her stories were difficult to believe.

'The trouble started in 74 when leaders of the left wing parties returned to Portugal from exile. After a while they formed a coalition Government with the armed forces and brought in land reform, a kind of purge on the wealthy. Anyone who owns land or business premises is under threat. They plan to take the land, especially if it's close to Lisbon.'

"But why does no one seem to know" I asked "Is it being suppressed?"

"If suppressed means held back, then it is"

A group of holiday makers at the next table looked startled, a waiter turned the background music up.

'The harassment starts in the middle of the night, with loud knocks on the door. When I open the door it's always the same- the police are standing outside holding a warrant... 'We have permission to enter' are the words they say. I don't reply. I stand back and let them enter. After marching in they look around then walk over to the electric meter 'Fascist' they shout 'wasting electricity.' Now I am too scared to put a light on. I use candles.'

"Why didn't Maria find somewhere else to live?" asked a worried looking Sue.

"The horses mean everything to her. The Coudelaria belonged to her parents; it follows a family tradition of only breeding from pure Iberian lineage"

"But when the Government wants land, you can't fight them" said a mortified looking Sue "This kind of thing can't be going on now... can it?"

"Although Portugal's not a democracy as we understand the word, it's getting there"

Following the tale of Maria, I walked the dogs down to the river in the gorge thinking the walk might help me relax. Why do things never run smoothly... And happen at the most inconvenient times?

After dinner, Geoff gives me one of his sideways glances. I can just see his eyes over his book. Inwardly I groan, it's a look I know so well. There's something he wants to say... Please don't let it be another shock.

"About your trip to Portugal..."

"I thought we'd agreed?" Why did I say thought? I'm putting words into his mouth; he could always say he doesn't remember agreeing.

"I just want you to be careful"

"I promise" I tell him, feeling relief flooding over me "Dad bought me a cheap flight out which also includes a hire car"

"When do you meet Maria?"

"Meeting her for dinner tomorrow, we've a lot to catch up on" Geoff was just being polite really. He'd said what was important. Dad and Geoff were similar. Both were on with the job men, small talk seemed to be a language they didn't understand.

"Sure you'll be alright?"

"I'd much rather stay at home, far too much to do. But give everyone my regards and bring back some training tips…"

*'Ask the wind how fast this horse can run.*
*For none can tell but the wind alone'*
*Al Andaluz.*

# 9. Meeting the Master… Step One.

*April 28 2 a.m.*

With a feeling of excitement I dressed, crept out of the house and walked into a chilly darkness. Outside was clear and still with an almost full moon. I could just make out a faint cone of sparkling lights above the eastern horizon. Geoff called the lights 'celestial fragments' he said they were particles of light from the zodiac.

"Amazing what you can see in high places" he said "I'm saving up to buy an astronomers telescope, then I can watch what's happening up there"

I suppose it was amazing, the lights disappeared if you looked from lower down the valley. For a long moment I stood very still watching the lights flickering, first to one side of the hills, then the other. Turning my back on the magic I walked to the land rover, not wanting to go anywhere except back to bed. I drove slowly until I reached the glaring illumination of Manchester's suburbia, then I moved along with the flow, slipping into the queue for airport bound traffic.

At seven fifteen I fastened my seat belt and watched the runway disappear into low cloud. After settling back in my window seat I reached for a leaflet, one of those glossy travel magazines the airlines put behind every seat. On the front cover were photographs of Gibraltar and South West Spain, on the back little known places in Galicia and Northern Portugal, dramatic scenes of cliffs rising out of the sea and forests tumbling down to the shore… Just looking at the photos brought back memories of Mums stories, the ones she told me when I was very young, fascinating stories of love and war,

Spanish horses and bravery. One of my favorites was the tale of Jebel Tarik.

"It all began in 711 A.D. when the Moors led by 'Tarik ibn Ziyad' occupied the rock of Gibraltar to launch the Islamic invasion of southern Spain. At the time Spain was weak from civil war and plagued by internal strife. Tarik, a Berber warrior took advantage of this weakness and chose the time to invade cleverly. Following his later success in Spain the rock was named 'Mountain of Tarik' or 'Jebel Tarik'.

The Moors also brought a number of fine quality Berber horses onto the rock of Gibraltar and then into Spain. They were handpicked and of the very best blood lines, showing great hardiness and courage. Pride and bravery seemed to be the most desirable qualities wanted in a horse – no horse could be too brave or too proud, and by careful cross breeding with the Spanish Horse, the Battle Horse of Kings reached its final form, he became the most wanted combat horse in Europe, and the most beautiful. But always remember - there is no permanence of breed characteristics…there is no permanence of anything really. You can buy it but you never own it. Either man or nature interfere, they always do. In todays world Battle horses are out of story books- Kings buy expensive racehorses or strings of polo ponies. And the selection that took thousands of years to perfect, is now no longer wanted"

An air hostess leaned towards me, she said "Please fasten your safety belt" My seat shook a little as the plane descended. I felt the pull of the earth and looked out into hazy cloud. Abruptly, thick cloud became blue sky and I gazed at the rock of Gibraltar towering high above the sea and over the surrounding countryside. The Mountain of Tarik was an intriguing place to be, a rock to fight for, where history had been made over and over again.

After a smooth landing the sun decided to disappear behind clouds, but only over Gibraltar and I began to wonder if there was something magical concerning the rock… I remembered Dad telling me about the rocks outline and height. 'The shape holds the clouds prisoners. If the top was made rounder and smoother, the clouds could drift away, but we can't do that, not where Hercules stood – so we have to keep the clouds.' After eating breakfast in the port, I walked across the border into the Spanish town of La Linea de la Conception, where I picked up my hire car and drove away following the Cadiz sign.

As I neared my destination, I pulled off the road. How could I drive past this point without feeling wonder? The sight of two continents' separated by only a few kilometers of sea... yet totally different worlds. The view never failed to thrill me. Over the water I looked at the Rif Mountains of Africa, the gleaming ultramarine of the Atlantic Ocean, and here where I stop to look out, I'm dazzled by the endless sparkling beaches and fields of wild flowers. This coast is a different Spain, it's a canvas of color called the coast of light and everywhere is flooded with brightness streaming down through a silver haze of white sand and shimmering sea. When I finally took my eyes away from the vivid colors, I tried to imagine what the Mediterranean valley might once have looked like, before the Atlantic Ocean smashed through the rocky Gibraltar Strait and flooded the land to form a sea. I pictured the early ancestors of the Iberian horse that came down to the valley to graze, the very first ancestors of Ganador.

'And the great rock barrier crashed open allowing giant waves from the Ocean Atlantic to submerge the low lying Valley Mediterranean flooding it yet again... Thus forming the Mediterranean Sea'

I stood on the very spot where European civilization started from, had evolved and developed into what we are now. As I gazed at the place 'where two seas mingle' I try to hold onto a dream, a towering rock - an icon from before time began, even older than the hills, ships passing through the Straits where the vast Atlantic merged with a tranquil sea. I remembered what Dad used to say, such beautiful words, and so true...

'Whenever two seas meet, the merging currents produce endless energy, create amazing cloud formations, and fierce electric storms'

I considered the idea behind these words, as I drove along the coast road towards my destination.... Tarifa, a Spanish town where history had been made over and over again, where vast stretches of white sand stretch out to greet the crashing waves of the Atlantic Ocean. Once there, I parked close to the beach and sat watching the enormous swell of the tide, just holding on to a dream.

At seven I walked up to the town, there was a blustery wind which hit me from every angle, made me long to enter the stillness of the old town with its high walls and narrow streets. I planned to meet Maria outside the wooden doorway into the old part, near the brass plaque, the one inscribed Puerta Jerez. I'd written the directions down in my diary when she phoned from the Lisbon Embassy where she worked as a translator. Maria never phoned me from home she worried that her own phone might still be tapped. But surely life was easier now? The political trouble started back in seventy four. Over five years had passed.

"Whatever are you doing in Tarifa?" I touched her shoulder, at first she looked startled and then she laughed. Nothing much had changed except her eyes; there was a sad look about them, a distant look.

"It's over the water tomorrow Norma, nine a.m. ferry - Tangiers. One of the officials needs a translator"

Arm in arm we strolled through a maze of narrow cobbled Calles. We walked under wrought iron balconies filled with flowers, stopped to gaze in pretty courtyards built around fountains which shimmered with Arabic tiles. An artist sat against the high wall of a church, he wrote poems in flowing Arabic symbols "Listen to this charming verse" said Maria and she translated the secret code of dots and squiggles.

*'In the old town fountains whisper*
*Gentle songs of Moorish Splendor*
*Murmur legends long forgotten*
*Paradise of singing waters'*

Presently we turned into a wider brightly lit calle; it was full of cafes and bars. The pavements were crowded, people standing everywhere even in the road.

At last we found a table in a Moroccan eating place down near the old castle. After ordering dinner we talked; we'd so much to catch up on and suddenly everything she'd had locked up inside came spilling out.

"Two men came to the farm – last week… They were looking at the breeding mares" She sounded hysterical, for the first time I could remember, there was a note of bitterness in her voice "A groom told me a dreadful story, he said there were rumors that breeding stock were being sold to the meat markets of France… Disappearing in the night"

"But can you rely on his words?"

"I don't know. I don't know anything anymore"

"But I thought the political games were over…?"

"I did too, but obviously not."

"Have you thought about moving out of the Alentejo?"

"It would be impossible to sell… A family of peasants fenced ten hectares off - started building a house, back in 75, the year of land reform – the deeds aren't worth the paper they were printed on"

"What does Enrique think?"

"Rico moved the Andrade stallions up North… His friends hiding them, in the stables of his hotel, the same hotel where we met. He's sending two of the mares up next week. I only hope it's in time. And then, he wants me to move into the hostel next door - thinks I'll go crazy unless I get away. 'Keep your head down he said– always act poor - watch the horses - and don't worry.'

"What are you going to do?"

"I've decided to get out… Until I know the horses and farm are safe. I feel as if I'm standing on the brink of a cliff, ready to fall off into a no man's land. Rico tells me I'll break down if I carry on worrying. I'm not me anymore, just an exhausted body going through the same old routines. Please Norma. Promise you would never disclose where we are"

"On my honor" I hugged her "Maybe you will have to go away. Don't ignore things until you fall off that cliff, will you?" She needed the rest - needed to get away from Lisbon, from the unhappy memories. What is it that causes some people to break, when others just carry on? I didn't know the answer, maybe nobody did.

"Police can't enter Hotels, or so Dad tells me. He said it could put tourists off… so the horses are safe"

"Your Dad told me that. He's so kind. But you can't imagine the worry"

"Oh but I can, very easily"

"When men taste anarchy and run wild, there's always a few who carry on as before, at least for a time. Anyway let's talk about you, and Ganador. Your Dad showed me some photos. Ganador has the same look as an Andrade line stallion. Big and powerful, the same look of dominance. Have you noticed Ganador always looks directly into the camera?"

"Yes I have"

"Supposed to show high intelligence"

Over dinner, we talked of my visit with the Master and what to expect.

"It's a great honor" she said "You will never forget him"

"Still can't believe I'm going" Suddenly I felt nervous.

"Perhaps Fernando mentioned you; or it could be Manuel, or maybe something you've written has caught his eye. Whatever it is, not many meet the Master"

"Feels like a dream, a frightening one. What if I can't think of anything half intelligent to say?" And we both laughed at the thought.

"Don't know of any English grooms wanting work out here do you? English grooms are worshipped here thought of as trustworthy and hard working" I think the wine must have loosened my tongue for I mentioned Sue's love affair with Spain and it's horses, told her Sue's plans and favored location.

"Spain and Portugal desperately want English speaking grooms" Oh dear I thought, what have I said? "If I hear there's anything near Seville, I'll do a spot of investigation. Find out what the yards are paying. Leave it to me" Maria searched for her diary, it was already bulging with information - and carefully found a spot for Sue's name.

"She will have no problem"

"But she's not available immediately" And then I realized, I should never have mentioned Sue in the first place.

*'In the name of land reform more than two million, two hundred thousand hectares of agricultural land were taken when leaders of left wing groups joined with the armed forces to form a coalition government during 1974 and 1975. Many of the finest Lusitanian lines became in danger when peasants took over the running of many Portuguese farms, losing hundreds of its finest specimens to the meat markets. However, due to the intervention of the Portuguese Government and the passion shown by some breeders, this very old and unique breed of Iberian Horse has returned to healthier numbers and is fast becoming one of the World's favorite breeds'*

# 13. The Master

*April 30.*

After spending two days braving Tarifa's winds, I leisurely began the drive to Lisbon Portugal, where arrangements had been made to meet with the great classical rider and ecuyer, Nuno Oliveira. I spent only one night in the city. At nine a.m. I headed for the bullring where the roads came together. It took a full hour to get out of Lisbon, there was a huge May Day rally - and I thought the trouble had finished, thought that freedom day had been and gone on April twenty fifth?  The crowds were enormous, I could hear names repeatedly shouted in a chant like rhythm– could it be a political meeting before a bullfight? But then I realized the time of day didn't fit in with my idea. At one point I thought the car might be attacked, there were figures surrounding it, fingers pressing on the windscreen, youth's raising placards... So stupidly I reversed, and a policeman ran towards me. Pretending I hadn't seen him I circled the nearby roundabout countless times until he went away.

With a sigh of relief I glanced at the road signs - right Lisboa, left Estoril, it had to be straight on.

Soon there was a signpost... it said Malveira, but the kilometer markings had been painted over. I stopped to look at the map, forty miles that was all.  I continued down the road, passing dilapidated farms and cottages. The road was empty except for a few donkey carts, delivering fire wood. I could tell the people were poor by the importance of this delivery – very poor. The older women stood in doorways - they wore black lace head coverings. Were they immigrants?

Within minutes I passed the fringes of the last wayside trees, and entered the rural community of Malveira, a quiet farming village set amidst peaceful countryside. Malveira to Mr. Oliveira's farm was then by way of a bumpy unmade road.

After seeming to drive for ages I saw a café sign, it swung in the breeze over the gateway to a stone house set amongst an orchard of lemon trees. The smell of newly baked bread and mouth - watering aroma of coffee overcame my fears and I ventured in. At the end of the path was a white painted arrow, it pointed to the back of the house where tables were set on the terrace overlooking the valley. The menu consisted of one dish, breakfast Portuguese style, whatever it was smelled delicious. A singing waiter walked over to my table, throwing his cloth over his shoulder he sang a verse from the opera 'La Traviata' in a rich tenor voice. He'd a lovely smile and sang in perfect Italian. The food could not have been more straightforward, freshly squeezed lemons from the trees around me, croissants straight from the oven, a pot of fresh coffee.

When I finished breakfast, the singing farmer had disappeared, standing in his place was a woman with sun bleached golden hair, she was very pretty, most probably his wife. She came and sat at the opposite side of my table, she stared at me enquiringly.

"Where are you going?" she spoke good English.

"Mr. Oliveira's – Is this the correct way?"

"You are not far from the boundary of his land, once it belonged to my grandfather" she smiled… And then I paid her.

"You must know the valley well" – I waited for the woman's reply. She stared at me in a curious way, I felt sure she looked amused.

"This valley is a very special place. Surely you can feel it?"

"I suppose I can" So I nodded pretending to understand, but I didn't… at least not yet.

"Everyone of us who lives in this valley knows the works of Verdi by heart… And that's no mean achievement" When she said these words, I thought there may be other singing waiters in the valley, but nothing more.

"But what is it that makes this place so very special?"

"Art" the woman said "The language of feelings, of emotion, it's all around me. When I listen to the music or watch the master riding I seem to enter another world, somewhere magical" The woman had said everything so eloquently. She had explained that nothing matters when surrounded by artistic genius. So true, an idea waiting to be set free by this country woman, an idea I would never forget.

She waved goodbye, and then turned to walk away, our conversation ended. I had been so wrong in thinking the woman still dreamed of the past, when the land once belonged to her grandfather, to her family. The peasant woman had got on with life, taken pleasure in all that surrounded her. I would never forget her words. Before I started the car up I felt sure I heard snatches of opera rising and falling on the breeze. Though distant and muted I definitely heard music, but then it disappeared.

Feeling excited I journeyed on, towards this other world, this magical world which I hoped would be Mr. Oliveira's ranch. The unmade track seemed endless, suddenly the track straightened – one last hill and I received my award for perseverance. At last I'd found Nuno Oliveira, the greatest classical trainer of all time…

*

'Here before me is the incredibly beautiful valley of Malveira, only forty miles from the bustle of Lisbon, but I could be in a different world.'
Diary

Suddenly I heard the strains of Italian Opera, soft and haunting, resounding over the fields, echoing into the valley. Here within surroundings of beauty and culture, where the music of Verdi played as if by magic stood the farm and riding school of the great classical rider Nuno Oliveira. As I entered the stable yard I immediately felt a sense of calm, of tranquility even. Since no one seemed to be about I tiptoed round the yard and peeped into the indoor riding school.

In the center of the school stood the master... Nuno Oliveira, giving a collective lesson in piaffer and passage. He stood quietly in the middle of the school, as if conducting an orchestra. Calling the name of a horse, he then commanded a movement, simply by the raising or pointing of his index finger. The horses responded first to their name, and then to his signal. All the horses were highly trained school masters with heaps more knowledge than their riders - they displayed the airs of high school effortlessly. I will never forget how thrilled the riders looked when each horse produced these difficult movements as if it had wings, without them having to do a thing. Nuno constantly reminded his class to 'relax and follow the movements' such a simple rule and yet so difficult to follow.

Suddenly he turned round and looked me straight in the eyes.

"Who are you?"

"I have an appointment my name is..." When he heard my name he smiled, and asked me if I wanted to sit in the gallery.

After the lesson I found Mr. Oliveira in his study, a small room only a few meters from the riding school. He sat at his desk writing - he asked me if I'd like to look round. The walls were covered in photographs, there must have been at least a hundred. Patiently he answered all my questions – sometimes he watched the progress of his young horses being ridden by students, from time to time he gave advice, 'lightness, rhythm and tact.' Nuno was the opposite of what I had anticipated, definitely not authoritarian but quiet and thoughtful.

His people skills were many; though slow to smile he had great perception and diplomacy his mild manner encouraging discussion. Nuno made it clear that he disliked any force or use of strength, his training aims being to establish 'lightness of contact and harmony with the horse'. Then he surprised me by asking about my horses. I told him about Ganador he wanted to know the name of the breeder and his lineage.

For Nuno dressage was a unique form of art, the objective; perfect understanding between horse and rider. He told me of his great passions, equestrian art and Italian Opera, especially the works of Verdi. He also told me of his dislikes.

'Equestrian art should not be an exhibition of movements obtained by constraint. Training is surely to conserve the horse's enjoyment in his work, and the horse cannot enjoy his work without the necessary suppleness, evenness of rhythm and brilliance?'

Nuno told me his training philosophy was really quite simple…"It is to allow the horse to work under the rider without tension. To allow him to enjoy carrying out all movements with physical brilliance, and mental calm, as though he is free…. Any constraint or force, reduces the energy he is willing to give to the trainer, until one day it is there no more"

After our conversation he invited me to stay for the afternoon and watch him ride. I felt very excited as I took my place in the gallery where at 3 p.m. Nuno Oliveira planned to display three of his horses. At that moment it became obvious Nuno was revered by students and experts from around the world. In the hum of chatter I heard many foreign students – I spoke to a French dressage trainer who introduced me to an American high school rider, but surprisingly there were no Portuguese or Spanish. My immediate neighbor turned out to be a Fellow of the British horse society who planned to spend his entire holiday studying Nunos training methods.

At 3.30 precisely a sudden silence descended on the spectators, all around I felt a sense of excitement, of expectancy. Everyone knew they were here to watch the greatest classical horseman of our time riding before them.

Before taking his first horse from the groom, he called for questions. Rudolf my BHS neighbor requested advice on training the young horse… length of training sessions and in particular contact with the bit. "Something every rider worries about."

Nunos response was immediate. "It is a great error to tire the horse; lessons must be short, for the more a horse is pushed… the more his energy is extinguished. It is also an error to sacrifice lightness of contact, riders who use force will never advance"

Rudolf leaned closer to my ear and whispered "Never sacrifice lightness… That's a good one… when todays riders are happy to carry a weight in both hands!"

A girl I recognized from the earlier class asked the next question,

"My horse is unreliable in sequence changes, either late or disunited. What should I do?"

"Then you must return to earlier work. A horse is not a machine" The great man replied to his pupil "Very rarely, will you be fortunate enough to work with a horse that progresses smoothly in its training… It is often necessary to repeat earlier training, time after time. Can the horse carry out the transition canter to walk with ease?"

"No, he refuses to walk"

"Then he does not understand or finds the work too difficult"

"But for how long?"

"As long as it takes – the horse must be a partner, never a slave"

Nuno placed a recording of Aida on the old fashioned record player he stood listening intently until satisfied as to the settings and volume of the music. Even the indoor school had charm, an elegance rarely seen in a riding school, Moorish style arches separated the gallery from the riding area, the Portuguese flag flew proudly, the walls were mirrored – some even decorated. In a corner stood a wooden chair and table, on the table a record player…

Now the Master is ready to ride I force myself to drag my eyes away, take out pen and notebook and prepare to describe everything before me. Maybe my writing will help me better understand this great mans technique?

The first horse was a four year old, cream colored, Lusitano stallion. For ten minutes he exercised the horse on the lunge line in the paces of walk, trot, and canter, without any side reins. What he did next more than surprised me- To the strains of Verdi's 'Love Duet' ringing out from the two riding school speakers, he attached side reins to the curb bit, encouraged a  collected trot, and immediately followed this, by requesting a few rhythmical steps of piaffe. Then with the hind legs active and engaged, he touched the horse with his whip. To my amazement the young horse displayed a high, spectacular capriole jump, possibly the most brilliant I had ever seen.

The second horse, a five year old bay stallion he also lunged before riding. Nuno began the mounted work by walking the horse through the lateral exercises of shoulder in, croup dentro, and half pass. A transition into canter revealed calm, well oiled pirouettes and neat rhythmical sequence changes. After the canter he resumed trot work, three trots were shown, working, collected and medium. At the end of the training session he worked from the ground on piaffe, aiming for transitions forwards into passage and to finish a little Spanish walk. At all times his contact with the bit was feather light, his aids invisible to detect. The horse obviously enjoyed his work, and moved with energy and brilliance. Throughout, there was a mental communication between man and horse, of a kind I had never before experienced. There existed perfect understanding and harmony between Nuno and his horses.

After changing the music yet again, he worked his final horse, a golden colored, fully trained stallion, which lifted his legs very high, and appeared extremely arrogant - possibly of pure Spanish origin. Once again the initial work was lunging; after which he worked the horse from the ground, on the short reins. The stallion displayed the airs of Haute Ecole with obvious enjoyment. He moved effortlessly, and with outstanding vigor, seeming always to be exactly in time to the music. Yet again I was to be surprised as Nuno rode canter in place followed by canter to the rear, each step on a feather light contact. Halting on x, he asked for six steps of piaffe which were developed into full pirouette left, and then right. To end the training session he worked on rein back, in a way I'd never seen before. The stallion stepped backwards across both diagonals, followed by half volte's in each corner, after that, the circle. Every step taken was calm, relaxed, and with rhythmical precision. This work to the rear was followed by riding school figures in collected trot, finishing with a spectacular extended trot, Spanish walk, and levade.

Sounding a lot braver than I felt, I asked Nuno Oliveira how classical equitation differed from the training aims of today.

"My wish is to establish a conversation with the horse.... A dialogue of question and answer, of courtesy and respect, which makes possible a greater interpretation of equestrian art"

At seven, I had to leave the fascinating world of equestrian art, Nuno Oliveira and his horses, promising to return in July.

At the bottom of the hill I stopped to listen to the faint sounds of music, coming and going on the warm spring breeze. Wiping away my tears I continued driving down the bumpy track towards Malveira village passing through its landscape of olive groves, and sweet smelling citrus trees. The sun was already setting in the west, and shortly my magical day would be but a dream. Sitting on a rock I watched the sun going down, before heading south to Lisbon. Finally, tired and weary I reached the airport where I bade farewell to my trusty hire car, joined the interminable queues, and started to look at my notes. After leaving the magical world of the Master I felt gloomy, everything around me seemed uninteresting and low key. What could I expect after a day in paradise? I will always remember the day I spent with Nuno Oliveira as a magical time; the time I saw a Grand Master of equestrian art, right there before my eyes.

*'Opera and equestrian art constitute a delicate balance between art form and energy, creating a spell of heightened awareness'*

# 11. Enter Xenophon

*Toby Jug Farm May 3.*

I arrived back from Portugal alive with excitement about meeting the great Master Nuno Oliveira... But when I saw Sue and Geoff I knew something was wrong. Geoff's carefree smile had disappeared - to be honest he looked miserable. And there was something else, the atmosphere felt edgy as if it were glued together and just waiting to fall apart. Sue quickly informed me of the cause, she couldn't wait.

"I've been offered a job in Spain Norma!" she screamed with what sounded to be delight.

"When do you start?" At this moment I was inwardly groaning. Maria hadn't wasted much time in finding Sue a job. I was seething with anger.

"The end of October and it's in Seville! A friend of Maria's rang only two days after you left"

Geoff said nothing. His silence spoke for him. He waited until Sue had gone up to her room before showing his annoyance.

"I didn't know anything about this" he stared at the floor, his face looked like stone.

"Maria doesn't care a hoot if we have no groom, all she cares about is pocketing commission... by supplying 'our' groom to somebody over there"

"I can't believe you actively promoted her. Grooms of Sue's competence don't grow on trees, especially in Spain" Geoff's voice sounded icy cold, and I waited for his temper to flare.

"Have you forgotten how long it takes to train anyone to be

remotely useful in a yard? Plus the need for constant supervision, if only to make sure the horses stay alive" he said in a razor sharp voice "And muggings me will be the supervisor- As far as I'm concerned, almost all qualified grooms need a further two years under lock and key" he shouted "Sues a damn miracle, and you arrange to send her to Spain, your unbelievable... blooming unbelievable"

There was nothing I could say, and this was one of the times not to try. I'd acted like a fool...so I stood there, bit my tongue, and waited for him to calm down.

So there it was... full circle, advertize for a groom, be seen to be making an effort, anything to calm Geoff down. This time there would be no excuses, and it was up to me to find a solution. Sue had only five months left at Toby Jug Farm; and I had exactly the same length of time, to locate and train a replacement - always assuming we were lucky enough to find someone suitable to train...

"What type of person are we searching for?" Sue asked one morning "May as well start thinking about priorities"

"If you think of a fearless Samurai wrestler you're on the right track" he replied before slamming the front door.

"I think Geoff has a point... not many are up to Ganador" all through his short life Ganador had been feared and condemned by many people, for the reason that he was not understood. Sadly much of his original softness and trust in humanity had turned into suspicion and distrust. Sue was correct - the choice of groom would most definitely be his, and not ours.

Only four and a half months are left with Sue at the helm- or to put it another way, one hundred and thirty days, until she leaves for Spain. This is a moment when I feel utterly miserable. I am in this situation just because I didn't think. Anyone with an ounce of sense would have found a new groom, long before they allowed Maria to enter Sue in her wretched diary.

*May 26.*
*'After four mind- numbing weeks of testing applicants I've started to feel stressed out, Geoff is probably correct, I must*

*be looking for the type of person who doesn't exist...'*

"Sue, please be honest" I said knowing that Sue would always be honest, even if it hurt "Do you think I'm looking for the unobtainable? All the grooms I turned away as dangerous or wooly headed would be fine working in a trekking centre?"

"Point taken" replied Sue over her book, "But this is not a trekking centre... is it?"

Suddenly her eyes widened "I've got it!" she said thumping the table as she searched for pen and paper.

"Listen to this Norma!" she said excitedly, "written by a long deceased guy name of 'Xenophon' 369 B.C. The attributes of a horseman... are...

To have a cheery spirit and never show anger

To be hard working.

Calm when faced by any sudden storms.

To possess sound nerves and sound body.

To have intelligence

To have patience

And to wind up: To love the horse and respect thy master."

"Oh yes, I'm writing the old guy's data down! This is where we have gone wrong – Don't you see? We should be rooting out personal qualities. Interviews and tests mean nothing to old Xenophon."

She carefully made a list of the qualities of a good horseman, promising to add a point's method so as to award marks... to any future candidates.

"I think the bit about 'respecting thy master,' will have to go... and 'hard working,' sounds rather like slavery... plus, 'calm in the face of storms,' is asking a bit much, the old guy possibly never knew what upsets were in the days of old." Sue was definitely on to something, or so she thought.

*"Excellent training maketh the horse,*
*For no horse was ever born vicious."*
*Xenophon.*

# 15. Kit and Michelle

*June 9.*

The following morning, there were three letters, two applications for the position of groom- which I quickly handed over to Sue and a third stamped Nuno Oliveira.

Dear Madam,

> I thank you for your interest in my work and bring to your attention that in the last excerpt from your series there is a caption describing the horse ridden by Mr. Manuel Sabino Duarte as an Alter Real. This seems unlikely since the pure strain of Alter Real's are bay/brown, and not grey.

I smiled to myself as I imagined the great man reading my appalling error, about the oldest and most famous Portuguese stud, a stud that had operated for more than two hundred and fifty years, headquarters of the National Stud nucleus of the Royal Riding School.

Nuno certainly couldn't wait to draw my attention to this unnoticed slip-up and rapidly my smile turned to humiliation.

> I suggest that you contact the Director of the Alter Stud, Alter do Chao, Alentejano. Who would be most happy to give you information on the breeding and training schemes of the stud. As you are interested in the classical school I suggest you contact Dr. Guilherme Borba head of Lisbons

Art Equestre which is at the Hippodrome do Campo Grande.
They work mostly with Alter Stallions and give full costume
displays (as seen in bullfighting) of High School Work. The
idea of the School is to preserve and present the traditional
work of the Portuguese High School. If there is anything else
I can help you with please contact....

I placed the letter on my desk, knowing I would now have to
write three letters, a thank you to Nuno, an amendment for the
magazine and a sorry to Manuel.

."Are you reading the application letters Sue? I don't want to
read them, especially at the crack of dawn"

"Hmm, listen to this!"  Sue spoke in a captivated voice
"Groomed at Fenwick's riding centre... and guess what else? You
will never believe this... has experience of grooming in a Circus,
name of Kit and aged twenty one. Perhaps he's with the lions!" Sue
said gleefully her imagination running wild as she thought of the
merits of a lion tamer.

"Oh yes; another good one" on reading the second application
her excitement grew.

"Now this girl sounds out- of- the ordinary. Reading between
the lines she requires a room with board plus training in caring for
horses, as mum is proposing a move to Scotland—And listen to the
next bit Norma,

"To train as an animal welfare officer following her training
here!"

"But why here?" I said not quite understanding the connection.

"Because she needs experience and knowledge of stallion care"
Sue banged the table in delight; "and listen to this Norma! She's got
experience helping with rescue cases in a horse's home – which
means she must be a caring type. Name of Michelle age twenty two
and with three 'a' levels to boot, can't be bad. These two give me a
good feeling"

"They sound fine on paper Sue," I said thinking of our
disastrous first twenty applicants... "But who are they in person?
What's behind the application - because up to now every letter has

proven to be damn well misleading?"

"But I have an inkling we are almost there, I can feel she's the one, I can feel it in my bones" replied Sue in her finest palm reader's voice.

"But where is there? Is it where we've ended on the past twenty useless occasions?" I answered sharply, completely failing to disguise my doubt and disbelief

Sue thought for a moment before replying,

"There… is the world of superior grooms, people who possess the 'attributes of good horsemen, surely you remember Xenophon Norma?"

And exactly two days later, it came to pass that Kit drove into the yard, completely unannounced. He drove into the yard sitting on a bright red moped which sounded like close range gun fire.

"Sorry about the noise of this thing" he shouted over his unsilenced engine, very slowly he removed his helmet, the offending din he left running "Thought I'd kill two birds with one stone; deliver dads football leaflets and find out where you lot are" he yelled towards Sue who was sweeping the yard.

"Turn the engine off" shouted a furious Geoff from the confines of the stable yard "Turn the key to its off position... I am trying to shoe a horse."

At last the explosions slowly fizzled out and I breathed a sigh of relief. The stillness of the moors made any man made noise agonizing.

"Are you Kit?" Sue asked, walking over to the offending red moped and the boy "If you are- better come with me"

"Right away" he replied "And sorry!" he shouted into the stable yard "My names Kit, or whatever else you care to call me!" all the while he grinned mischievously. Sue never disguised her hatred of bad manners and glared towards him "Sorry folks, just one of my little jokes!" Kit hurriedly tried to explain his actions away after considering the look of contempt upon Sues face.

"Norma" called out Sue, "There's a 'boy' here, name of Kit. "Do you want to see him… or not?"

If only I had said no, but I said yes in a brainless gesture of goodwill.

Ganador took on a look of amazement when he set eyes on Kit with his black curls and amusing tone of voice. Maybe he thought Mark had returned? But, Kit passed the practical tests by the skin of his teeth, despite persistent talking.

No doubt the stallion would form his final judgment in due course, but up to then I found Kit to be an affable lad with a cheery smile and a ceaseless flow of chatter. He seemed so helpful, his smile so charming.

"I'm hard working and I never panic" he said hesitantly. After the first would be 'grooms' he seemed to be a miracle. Only Sue had reservations…

My interview with Kit began well, but then became rather hazy as Kit did most of the talking. However, it was manifestly clear that Kit enjoyed being with horses and had a passion for Circus.

By the end of our 'talk,' I knew exactly where he delivered the football coupons, how much money he earned for delivering them, the names of his favorite liberty horses, how to clean a tigers cage out safely and how one day he wanted to work full time in the Circus.

Every question he answered appeared to be woven together by the golden threads of what Kit really wanted to say, and not what I wanted to know.

"There's just one problem" said Kit "I promised to help out at Circus Winter Quarters on two days a week, Saturdays and Sundays. The animals that are not travelling are kept on a Cheshire farm; giraffes, elephants, tigers and horses."

"What kind of things are you helping with Kit?" I said, recalling Sue's visions of a lion tamer

"Only mucking out and cleaning pens," Chris said happily.

I felt dubious about Kit; even though he didn't seem to possess the qualities of a good groom, he appeared very enthusiastic about coming back. And if I was completely honest… he'd been the best out of a bad bunch, so far.

Promptly and confidently Kit suggested he could return on

Monday morning.

"Please don't allow me to inconvenience you, but I have learned more about horses in half an hour here than in two years at the other place." He was doing it again, weaving in those golden threads of meaning and saying only what he wanted to say and hearing only what he wanted to hear.

I must be mad I thought, Kit had directed the interview and was now arranging to come back on Monday; quite an achievement for an applicant not yet contacted.

Being a coward I agreed he could work alongside Sue on Monday morning. After all, how could it harm discovering extra details about the real boy? Learning more about his capabilities when preparing feeds, his observance of safety rules such as closing doors and bolt's? Furthermore, Ganador's final decision was not yet known, and that would be very interesting.

Later that morning I asked Sue what she thought of him. "How do you rate him?"

"He's exasperating… I feel there's something missing if you understand me"

"But what were his marks?"

"His attributes mark is half a point; which I gave for his steady smile. Regarding his cheeriness of spirit we shall have to wait until Monday. Just imagine going through it all again, listening to his yapping, he never stops. I do hope he thinks as rapidly as he talks"

Monday dawned clear and bright, and Sue went out to do battle with Kit shortly before nine a.m. On returning to the house, for mid morning coffee Sue flopped into a chair and sighed, she looked tired.

"Norma, please listen" she almost pleaded. "He's fine mucking out and swilling down; that is when he stops talking for long enough to hold the pitchfork. But any job requiring thinking is beyond him. The boy never learns. Small things such as weighing food or soaking linseed seem to be completely beyond him. I showed him how to weigh feeds on FOUR occasions and he still did not have a clue! I'm not fencing with words Norma, please believe me. He is very cheerful but appears to possess absolutely no intelligence, which means he requires watching. Plus, he never stops talking, yap, yap, yap." Sue spoke hurriedly before the boy returned to the house.

"Nevertheless I have to admit that Ganador tolerated him, which was surprising really. Funny thing was, he only put up with the boy in small doses! Allowing him to do whatever was necessary, preferably as quickly as possible and then get out!" the coffee appeared to be calming Sue, helping her to see the humor within the situation.

"How did the stallion show his impatience?" I asked hoping he had not bitten Kit at such an early phase.

"Usually Ganador favored sharpening his teeth on the stone wall rather than eating his hay. The boy laughed at his 'antics' until I told him to remove himself from the box, quickly."

At that moment I saw Kit walking past the window and rapidly changed the subject.

"Would you like coffee with sugar Kit?" I asked, hoping our chat on the subject of himself had not been overheard.

"I'll have everything that goes with it please Norma" he said in a quiet voice.

After coffee and biscuits Kit came into the kitchen, he said in a delicate tone of voice "Norma can we speak privately?" On hearing the word 'private' Sue immediately stood up and returned to the stables.

"This has made me realize how much I have to learn," he went on "Please let me work here every Monday and Wednesday?" his voice was very persuasive. "Please, I promise to be quiet as a mouse."

"Yes of course," I heard myself saying "If you promise to be hard working and help Sue and Geoff."

Perhaps I should have learned from my recent experiences and said 'No.'

Even now I wonder why I agreed and said "See you on Wednesday and bear in mind you work under Sue and Geoff, as a general help."

Our next applicant, number twenty two arrived in the yard the following morning, exactly on time. The moment I saw Michelle I felt she was a young woman worthy of the position.

She was the kind of person who exudes confidence to all around her; she possessed a certain charm or poise with a let's get on with it style. There seemed to be an aura of buoyancy about her, with confidence to spare. Peculiar, bizarre, call it what you like…but after spending four weeks of seeing absolutely no-one who even came near to being suitable, here was the perfect groom. Simultaneously everything seemed to be happening together!

Michelle passed all the practical tests easily; strangely Ganador ignored her, and refrained from his acts of terror. At the first sight of her blonde curls and very calm voice he and the others became happier horses and I discovered that there may well be light at the end of the tunnel.

"I can begin on the last day of October," she said on consulting her diary "The society insists that I need working experience with stallions and large animals. In addition, I must pass my driving test and then I apply for officer training." This young lady was ideal for the position and I felt incredulously glad to offer her the groom in residence position, even if it was for only a year. Now only one small problem existed, and that was Kit, would Michelle want Kit working alongside her on two days a week - was it fair to even ask her?

"Would you mind a boy helping?" I asked bravely "Only two days each week…Works with the circus and he loves horses"

In a quiet yet tenacious manner, she said exactly what her plans would be - and for a moment I held my breath.

"Don't worry" she said "Another pair of hands is always a help!" Michelle could not have understood the politics of the situation - maybe she had a different line of attack?

"He is very talkative, like all teenage boys his mind seems frequently to be somewhere else." I felt a responsibility to add this last remark… And then she unveiled her approach.

"I can always find him lots of heavy work" she looked back at me, I felt sure she looked amused "It's the most sensible approach" she suggested, her eyes twinkling "Most boys are a lost cause you know!"

"I suppose your right" I conceded as convincingly as I could. The thought of Kit doing heavy work was unimaginable, but if it kept him away from the horses and her, it was a brilliant idea. Why hadn't Sue thought of it?

If she had only known how correct her theories were on so many things she may well have said no, but she said yes and so Michelle or Shelly became our new groom!

So there it was; everything had in the end concluded perfectly. We had the promise of a groom, plus a helper.

Sue and I smiled blissfully as Michelle departed up the track with mother.

"I knew it!" said Sue "I knew that someone was waiting out there for this little job, someone from the world of good grooms. I told you Norma" she spoke in a victorious tone of voice. Later that same day Sue brought her marking cards downstairs for me to see, before they met their end in the bin, and only one person, that person being Michelle had gained the obligatory ten points to be termed a horseman with the required attributes.

'Cheery of spirit and never angry: always calm, healthy body with nerves of steel. Intelligent and patient: a love of the horse and a wish to learn more.' I noticed the tenth commandment; 'serving thy master' had been changed to the word 'trustworthy.'

Unfortunately Kit had gained a meager one and a half points... But he was still in second place. He was awarded half a point for his cheery smile, but nil for spirit. Zero for never angry or hard working, with the words 'unless constantly supervised,' written in the mark box. 'Becomes stressed out' had been written over calm, with an additional half given for sound in body though not in nerves. Never uses his intelligence and does not possess the virtue of patience, were written in the subsequent mark box. An additional half point had been given for love of the horse, with the comment 'loves some more than others.'

Nevertheless, obtaining one and a half points placed Kit in

second place out of a field of thirty applicants, not bad!

Therefore, thanks to the knowledge and insight of a remarkable horseman living more than two thousand years before, I at last know the attributes of the perfect horseman. The observations of who will remain closely by my side.

*The race is not to the swift, nor the battle to the strong.*
*Ecclesiastes 9:11.*

# 16. Ganador's Invitation

*July 14*

As Sue began to pack, I dreamed I was back in Seville... I imagined the palm trees sparkling and shimmering in Louisa Park as they always did when darkness fell. The night air... heavy and sweet with the perfume of oranges and plants of the night...

Everything had been arranged, this was the end of an era, the last Friday of October would be Sues final day... In a way I felt jealous... I loved Seville.

"I told you Norma that everything would finish smoothly in the end, didn't I?" Already Sue had started to pack, she was filling an assortment of bags, with knitting patterns and balls of wool, others with various sizes of needles... wherever Sue went, so did her knitting.

"I adore this feeling. I'm free and happy and wish it could last forever... Whatever happens during the next six weeks will not stop me dreaming of Seville. Sounds just like paradise." She didn't listen for my reply "The memo on my agenda this week is the arrival of the plane ticket, and it's a one way. I'm so excited! Let's have a natter about Seville...Tell me what to expect"

"For me, it's a city of dreams, I love every inch of Seville. It isn't important politically or culturally, but it's rich in color and excitement, especially at night"

"But where should I plan to visit first?"

"The Alcazar... To feel it's magic. Then you should stroll by the river, the east side and then the west. Enjoy the atmosphere, learn about the early civilizations that lived and loved there, from before five thousand B.C. Long ago, Seville would resemble an empty canvas, and then each passing culture has painted its very own personnel brush strokes, to make it what it is today... One of the world's greatest capitals.

I love to walk by the river and visit the cafes in the old town... watch people dancing sevillanas in the streets until early dawn. Seville's a city of the night, a wonderful city, there's no denying it. There's something to make everyone happy in Seville, and it always finds something to celebrate. The city is vibrantly alive, and oozing with history and fine horses. At Easter, Seville opens the series of Spring Festivals, it's followed by Jerez's 'Week of the Horse'... where you can still see Baroque style dressage performed. The local's love it... The old techniques have never been completely replaced by modern styles – not in this corner of Andalucia."

"Whatever does Baroque style dressage mean?"

"It means riding in the Andalucian manner, how it used to be, which means everyone does what suits him best, showing off to the best of his ability. The men love to show off; the main thing on their agenda is the applause of the crowd. Anything and everything can go into a display. Tricks like bowing, and spinning pirouettes - the whole performance is like a game, light hearted- but deadly serious. You should hear the comments, and suggestions, passing backwards and forwards between riders and spectators."

"Sounds different to our dressage, more like circus"

"I suppose it is like circus, except the horses enjoy themselves. Mostly, the riders are made up of Picadors, who normally perform their antics in the local bullring – with the addition of a few brilliant Haute Ecole riders, who choose to turn out only to the grand Ferias of Seville and Jerez!

Mum and Dad always visit the Festivals... they love the atmosphere. At Jerez, last year there was a competition to find the horse which took the longest time to travel the length of the main street.

The winner enjoyed a wonderful half hour in snail's pace passage, where every step of the way the horse was admired, and encouraged to lift his legs higher. The crowd gets as much pleasure from seeing the horse, as the rider does riding it. You're in for a culture shock."

"But isn't too much collection harmful?"

"It's extremely hard on the hocks, fetlocks and everywhere behind the saddle, but this way of moving has woven its way into Iberian culture, and is seen as beautiful - by some"

"But how and when did this change begin?"

"It all started when King Philip V came to the throne, he was French - and he was a man who didn't like bull fighting"

"What a kind man he must have been"

"But his kindness had a repercussion on the type of horse bred within Spain. The strong fighting horse began to be bred only for the beauty of his head and neck, and long silken mane. No longer was he selected for his abilities in fighting; only his beautiful forehand became important. And then - during the last century he was used to pull small carts during the Ferias of Sevilla and Jerez. To pull at a very energetic trot but following a walking horse carrying a girl, side seated. The noble Spanish Andalucian had to do his best to waste his energy by making the most energetic steps upwards and sideways... but never forwards. So after centuries of careful breeding, the most wanted fighting horse in Europe gradually became a caricature of his former self... beautiful, but a horse suitable only for parade"

"Why does man always interfere, usually not for the best?" asked Sue.

"That's a characteristic of man! Though thankfully a few of the older Spanish lines were still left untouched... but you can never undo what's been done, not completely" At that moment the letter box clanged, Sue ran to get hold of the post before the dogs did. As she walked back into the kitchen she was smiling for the world.

"It's finally here!" she screamed with delight "My air ticket." She was bubbling over with joy "And something for you Norma, perhaps it's Fernando's letter?"

For a few moments I gazed at the impressive Portuguese stamp, and then resolutely decided to open the letter later, when together with Geoff. But curiosity won the day, I found it impossible to resist such temptation, and after one savage tear, I opened the envelope. After all I had waited four weeks, and not many people ever received seriously long letters from Fernando.

"Frame it Norma! I mean of course frame it after Geoff's read it. Tell me what he has to say, please?"

I kan understand the problems! Ganador is of pure Spanish lineage. It is not surprising that his past experiences have created unsoundness, and a very anxious horse? In order to understand the old classical methods it is necessary to know a little about the horse that high school airs were first materialized for. The Spanish Horse, a horse exactly like Ganador, a horse with many differences to other breeds both physically and mentally.

A Spanish horse meant horses that are bred within the Iberian Peninsular. Whether they be Lusitano or Andalucian is immaterial, they are Spanish and are genetically similar.

The name depends on the area where they are bred. Within Spain they used to be bred for 'Parading' in trot, sometimes Haute Ecole, now the Spanish are breeding a horse more suitable for the present, they call it the Pure Raza Espanol. Within Portugal they are bred for equestrian bullfighting or sport horses.

The politics of Spain have meant the importance of breeding a fine parade horse, very high stepping in trot, with a shorter action. The Andalucian was the ideal horse for military parades, whilst the politics of Portugal always favored the breeding of the equestrian bull fighting horse, the Lusitano.

The Iberian horse is the oldest saddle horse known to man, used for combat, referred to by Homer, and seen in cave paintings as early as the 111C B.C.

So, to begin retraining we work towards the basic foundation of strengthening and making supple, building up ze back muscles by working on the lunge in the long low outline. The minutes given for exercises must never be exceeded, as damaged muscle or ligament tires more quickly. Never ask for more than he is capable of giving, never! The muscle has not been allowed to stretch only to contract, slowly becoming starved of oxygen. But day by day we try to reverse the process up to when he is stronger with more impulsion.

Never forget that most resistances or disobediences are usually caused by stiffness, often unsoundness, within our horse, therefore it is a test of our training to always be ready to be sympathetic towards our colleague the horse.

Some of my horses, perhaps horses with problems, only work in collection twice a week for a maximum of thirty minutes. They are lunged on alternate days, turned out for a run daily or taken out for a walk.

Remember the Spanish horse finds collection easy, therefore collection must not be introduced too early, as Ganadors was. The 'non' Spanish horse finds collection difficult! With the non Spanish horse I aim to be quick to reward; a few steps of collected trot after our medium trot is excellent in training for it is always important that we understand the abilities of our horse and then train with this in mind.

We must always reward as certain horses like certain people, need to be rewarded more favorably or frequently than do others!

The problems you will encounter will be many, changing frequently from day to day.

Not surprisingly problems are many due to conformation or unsoundness; there are many horses such as Ganador with stiff painful back muscles, or are weak behind. But always remember the power to move forwards begins in the hind legs, the horses engine is powered from behind the saddle.

I kan refer to only a few problems: there are poor forehands, shoulders not free enough, neck too short or too long, fusion of spinal bones, problems in the stifle or hock, poor quality hooves.

Remember that bad training or training too quickly, without the basic work of impulsion and suppleness always breaks the horse down early or creates a nervous sometimes violent animal. Why? The horse thinks he cannot please his master, for we promote stiffness and tension through not moving forwards. Also we must be sure he understands? Does he flex to each hand, or move away from either leg? Kan he keep straight if worked away from the boards- and if not why not?

You must remember Norma to constantly watch your horse, for if he looks more beautiful his training is most usually on the correct lines.

Weaknesses can sometimes be trained into strengths, but only if we show great patience and do not expect too much exertion. We try to lessen the amount of exertion the horse uses by teaching transitions and differences within the pace, slow walk, to more lengthened walk, balanced trot to a more lengthened trot.

We must compare a young horse with weaknesses or defective conformation to a small child who has to do physiotherapy exercises to help build him up and free his movement.

With care, tact, patience and knowledge of when to ask, or when to finish or change the work, we kan at times, greatly improve him.

Never forget that training is about obedience. Training the movements should however never exceed ten minutes to be followed by straight forward work, which is directed at achieving the horse's fitness. Work which is relaxing, balanced trotting on straight lines, walking on a long rein cantering large circles, We kann of course repeat our ten minutes of schooling on figures or in collection when our horse is relaxed, but only if the horse is not tired. The horse will tell us when he is tired as not surprisingly he will find many problems when he becomes tired, this is why the straight forward work which is directed at improving his fitness is so important. Then we must rest the horse.

Remember that the horse must be 'relaxed' and mentally

kalm for if there is tension there is no training. The rider also must also be relaxed! Of course we often see horses forced to perform school figures when tense; but a horse with stiff muscles is in a state of tension and will very quickly injure himself.

I am at great pains to point out that when the kalm is lost, no beneficial training can proceed. Too much collected work or when collection is requested in the wrong manner as with much piaffe tells us that he may never be completely kalm ever again.

But the 'golden rule' in any training is to maintain the kalm of the horse, then ride him forwards teaching him straightness. Only then kann he use himself as the rider desires and perhaps obtain some lightness.

Kalm, forwards into straightness and eventually light…

I read the letter once more before placing it back into the envelope, and handing Fernando's treasured words over to Sue. His expert knowledge and sympathy with the Iberian horse always amazed me. His words were usually unanticipated. One way or another, Fernando knew everything about his subject… not only was he a worldwide authority on the Iberian horse, classical training and horse breeding… he was also an international dressage judge and the son of the late Ruy D'Andrade, one of the greatest historians to have lived.

Sue read Fernando's letter a second time whilst I sat thinking about its contents. In the letter there was a vast amount of knowledge, history, training techniques, philosophy, and of course, common sense. I intended to read it again and again- and afterwards use it for reference.

"Not many people know someone like Fernando Norma, I wonder if he needs a groom?" pondered Sue. "What if I'm not happy in Seville?" She spoke in a hesitant way, her tone of voice ringing with uncertainties concerning her adventure into the unknown.

"After living on the Yorkshire moors, Seville has to be a

paradise" But I knew how unsure she must be feeling; she was moving forever closer to the unfamiliar, worries about the unknown were beginning to multiply.

Sometimes I wondered, if she'd miss the hills, and the moors, the splendor of the landscapes, the tranquil calm. No amount of shopping in designer stores could ever compare to seeing the warm glow of purple heather, casting its haze over the valley, or the sounds of hawks screaming in the gorge. There was something hypnotic about living in the clouds.

I remembered the week after we moved into the farm.... "Come quickly" Geoff had shouted "I'm in the stable yard" When I ran outside, I was hit with a weird sensation, as if I was airborne. Looking down, I saw an endless sea of startling white cloud tops floating over the valley... There were millions. The farm stood in an empty void, all on its own. It seemed like an incredible dream, the kind of dream that recaptures something you never really understood.

"I feel like I'm flying" I said "This is the view from a plane window... its wonderful"

"But we are here, in the stable yard and standing here doesn't cost anything" Without cloud cover the sky gleamed a metallic blue... the brightness hurt my eyes,  far too dazzling to even gaze at.

"I feel as if... I'm walking on clouds" I would never forget that day. I only hoped Sue had good memories to take away. As if reading my thoughts she suddenly said,

"Do you know Norma; I think I may possibly miss this place..."

*

After tea the telephone rang. Sue went to reply, it was on its fourth ring when she answered.

"Just a minute" she turned round with a look of surprise "Norma" she hissed across the room "It's for you- a man from a scrap yard and his name is Adams" she covered the mouthpiece "Maybe it's 'him'... the Gypsy?"

"After all this time" I said "Wonder what he wants?" And Sue pressed the receiver into my hand.

"Hello... Norma speaking"

"It's Adams here... from the scrap yard surely you remember the day you bought Ganador?" I closed my eyes in trepidation.

"I'll never forget the day..."

"We've missed him so we have – Mother and Mark wept the day Ganador left. But I'm ringing about a happy event I'm inviting Norma, Geoff and Ganador to Marks wedding"

"You want to invite Ganador to Marks wedding?" Now I felt surprised.

"He's number one on the guest list, so he is. At a Romani wedding, a white stallion of the likes of King Ganador is a blessing from the God's. Mark loved the Oss. He never got over losing Ganador – never. I'll make it worth Geoff's while. Everything has a price so it does"

I thought of Geoff's hurt pride over losing his three hundred pounds to Adams, and quickly changed the subject.

"What's the bride's name?"

"Evita... she's a Spanish Lass, a real beauty, He met her at Appleby Fair" For a moment I felt sure he was holding his breath as he waited for my decision.

"There's a spare bedroom in the living wagon and a stable for Ganador. Mother says you're more than welcome." He was pleading now – so I replied.

"I'd love to accept the invitation... providing Geoff agrees, and Ganador walks into the box..."

*'The world is like a dancing girl, it dances for a little while*
*to everyone.'*
*Arabic*

# 17. Mark's Romany Wedding

*August 1 1980*

So arrangements were made to attend Marks wedding, Sue insisted on skipping her weekend break and Geoff finally agreed to drive the horsebox.

"Not many people are invited to a Romany wedding – You must go. Just imagine, for one day in his life… Ganador is a blessing from the God's. I told you it was like a fairy story, and now it's even better." Sue beamed with happiness as she waved us goodbye.

The horsebox trundled up the track on its second journey to the scrap yard. The time was 8 a.m. when Geoff turned into the moorland road, not a trace of mist was in sight. I could see for miles over the moors, it was a beautiful day with not a cloud in sight.

"Ganador walked straight in when no-one was about. He was perfect" Geoff said proudly "Different to the last fiasco"

"Remember March" I asked "The freezing fog and black ice?"

"I won't forget that drive in a hurry – Daylight and good visibility always help" And so they did, for the journey seemed much easier than the previous one.

At four a.m. we passed the White Horse Inn, and there it was, the hand painted sign, hanging from a nail in the half dead tree.

"Exactly as I remember it"

"Not with balloons attached though" added Geoff with a hint of surprise.

On turning down the track, I was surprised to find still yet more signs of festivity, balloons floated from the industrial colored hedge… and the gate to the yard stood wide open. At both sides of

143

the entryway were flowering ornamental trees in hand painted pots, and for a moment the gloomy yard looked almost inviting.

"Life's full of surprises" muttered Geoff as he turned into the yard "Some-ones been working hard" The piles of scrap metal which once concealed the living wagon had gone, and in their place were rose bushes and pots of geraniums. It was then I first saw Adams… heard his greeting.

"Welcome to my palace" he beamed and gave a little bow… I'd forgotten some of his mannerisms "Mark" he shouted "Ganador's back!"

Mark came running from the direction of the paddock, he looked glad to see us and in a way I felt happy to see him. He shook Geoff's hand in the manner of travelling people, thumbs on top, elbows touching, followed by a slap on the back.

"Geoff Lad!" said Mark "Tis good to see your face… How's Yorkshire…and Ganador?" After a little while he acknowledged my presence, turning his head he winked and looked me in the eye "And Norma of course" and then he grinned, he was just as I remembered him, charming, boyish, and Gypsy all the way through.

I knew the men greeted each other first, ignoring the women until later – this was their way. The traveller's world was a man's world – men drank together…laughed together… Women took a back seat, they cooked, cleaned, bore children, looked pretty – but never crossed the dividing line that separated male from female, neither did they share in the camaraderie of the men.

After unloading Ganador, Adams slowly walked round him, all the while keeping a safe distance from his teeth.

"Yorkshire air's doing the Lad fine, so it is" At the sound of his voice the stallions ears flattened back.

"Tis Geoff's feeding Dad… Horses don't live on air, no matter how fresh it is" Mark laughed at his father's remark "Go and put the straw down, the Lad wants a good thick bed" The men led Ganador down to the ramshackle cabin, a place I never thought he would return to. In the distance I listened to their voices laughing and talking, probably about horses or Appleby fair. They would talk, until it came time to visit the Pub.

When the men had gone, Mother told me the story of Evita…

"Beautiful girl – she's very young, but that's the way with travellers"

"Adams tells me she's Spanish"

"And so she is… her family own two flamenco bars… ones in a place called Triano Barrio, used to be the Romany part of Seville, the others in the center of Granada, a kind of nightclub. Marks a lucky lad – he's marrying into money! The girls family are over from Seville – plus a flamenco group, you'll be meeting them tomorrow"

"Whatever was Evita doing in England?"

"Each year her father drives from Seville to Appleby fair – calls it his holiday. The two fell for each other the time Adams took Ganador to the fair… and when they met again… that was it, ring on a finger!"

"So Ganador has been to Appleby fair?"

"The man at the big house wanted rid of him; he said the horse had too many problems. It broke my heart thinking I'd never see Ganador again. But they brought him back; and Mark found a bride"

"Wonder why Ganador wasn't sold. I know the Romany's love Spanish horses"

"They all wanted him Lass, but no-one had the funds to buy him. You see Adams set a price that nobody could afford. He doubled the price he was told to ask" There wasn't much I could say to that, so I changed the subject to the wedding.

"Is a Romany wedding ceremony different to a normal one?"

"I'd be a liar if I said no" she laughed "Just enjoy it and don't worry your head about what you can't understand, because the ceremonies based on traditions, thousands of years old… and it's Spanish, which means anything can happen"

"But where does Ganador come in?"

"White horses have always been worshipped for their spiritual qualities. From the earliest days, there's evidence that only white horses, were allowed to pull the chariots of the God's." And she picked up a history book and read out these words "Eight white

145

horses were kept to draw the holy chariot of the God Zeus, in the time of Xerxes…"

"I had no idea about these stories" After the long journey Mothers lilting accent caused me to feel sleepy… and my head started to nod.

"Don't fall asleep Lass, I've another tale yet. The story of the holy white horses" She closed the history book and spoke very slowly "Long ago, when the great flood covered the land of Mesopotamia…. At the same time that Noah called the animals into the Ark two by two. Only the Unicorns refused to enter the Ark, they preferred playing in the water, rearing and plunging and trying to fly. From that day on, these creatures were known as Holy White Horses."

"But why are they holy?"

"Unicorns are holy because they missed getting into Noah's Ark, missed the chance of reproducing their own species. It's all to do with virginity Lass"

"I think I understand… Except for the word white"

"The color white is from the sea spray as it touched the hair of their manes and tails, shining and glinting in the light… From then onwards called white, and this is the origin of the legend of the holy white horses.

After I wed Adams one of the Romany elders took me aside and told me this story, she said that I must always remember virginity symbolizes holiness. She alleged that some Gypsy women prevent their daughter's from wearing white, until the day they wed.

The Romanies and tradition are one, they'll never be parted, never… And it's all because of the holy white horses… Are you beginning to get the idea?"

"I'll always remember the origin of the word white"

"You'll imagine the Unicorns Lass; and the foam from the sea spray sparkling in the light" I took a deep breath, and asked Mother how she met Adams.

"I'm not Romany – not that I've anything against the community. My family live in Ireland, and that's where I was bred and born.

We met in Dublin at the annual horse fair... Adams married outside as they say" she sighed "Outsider's never fit in to the travelling life – never. And Roms never accept outsiders." she said sadly.

"But you married outside"

"I married in Ireland, there's a sea in between Lass"

"So nobody knows you're an outsider"

"Some things are better not known. But for Mark this marriage would have broken up long ago...it's a lonely life for a woman, if she's not with the clan."

After lunch the following day, a never ending procession of Romanies began to arrive. Two large living wagons pulled onto the paddock followed by a convoy of shiny four wheel drive motors, towing trailers and caravans.

From the moment they entered the yard, any calm moved out, there was laughter, chatter, and the clinking of gold.

Everyone had dressed in their finery, with masses of jewelry.... Gold flashed everywhere, some wore lots of rings... on every finger, and the smell of perfume was intoxicating.

In dress the men appeared comparable, in a flashy kind of way – tight black trousers, open neck silk shirt, and high heeled flamenco boots - black curls greased, and swept back in pony tails.

The young women wore brightly colored dresses of silk, with the shortest of skirts, and low, revealing bodices glittering in sequins.

Some of the more mature women were dressed in the old style... Long swirling flamenco dresses, hand painted fans and fine lace shawls. They were excited about the wedding and looked so very colorful that I felt out of place. Compared to them, I looked dull and uninteresting. When not one more guest could squeeze into the scrap yard or park on the adjoining field Mother insisted it was time to meet Evita's parents.

"They want to meet you" she said "Without Ganador this ceremony would be but a sham. Not many Romanies have a Ganador to bless the wedding" Through Ganador I'd been welcomed into their private world, seen a way of life I never knew existed, learned of ideas and customs I didn't understand.

As we neared the living wagons groups of women turned and stared in my direction. I felt nervous and excited both at the same time.

"They are not of your race" Mother placed her arm round my shoulders as though feeling my unease "Gypsy women are suspicious of any stranger" And then she nudged me…

Mariapi stepped down from the first living wagon, she walked towards me her arms outstretched and the Gypsy women fell silent waiting to hear her voice.

"My names Mariapi, I'm Evita's Mother" She looked too young to be the mother of the bride. She was small slim and hauntingly beautiful, but in a wild, natural way.

Her glossy red black hair cascaded in ringlets to below her waist, her eyes were set wide apart and sparkled as black as jet "You must be wondering how we know Ganador?" Quickly I decided to say nothing about what his first owner told me.

"I don't know much of his past" She smiled at my ignorance and twirled a pirouette, as only a dancer could.

"No, how can you?" Her every word sang, her movements pulsated with a rhythm that surged through her body. How could I understand what made her different? As Mother said I was not of her race.

Just then I heard a man's voice, sitting on the first step of the wagon he sang flamenco cante – there was a mysterious quality about his voice that made his song unlike any cante I'd heard before.

His voice was full of passion, a restrained passion. It was harsh and vibrating but it arose spontaneously and seemed to express his innermost feelings.

"Pepe's telling you of the sorrows and joys of life- you must shout olé" whispered Mother with a wink.

"Why must I shout olé?"

"Because his song is for you"

A few minutes later we sat together in the living wagon where

Mariapi continued her story of Ganador's past.

"When the moon was full the Master's greatest pleasure in life was to ride in his carriage through Sevilla, Ganador and his brother Papillon pulled his carriage and as manager of his Yeguada Pepe would drive. He trusted Pepe with his horses- you see those two horses were the finest driving pair in Spain. Always he requested the same route – down past the beautiful gardens of the Alcazar where the horses moved slowly and in step, almost piaffe, which gave the carriage an illusion of moving but advancing little. Antonio wished to linger and dream of the past, he loved to watch the dancing lights on the Alcazar's walls he called the golden glow 'the sunlight of the night.'

After the Alcazar Pepe would drive into Santa Cruz, through a warren of white alleyways, under flower filled balcony's… People crowded outside the bars trying to touch the horses for luck. Ganador loved those nights, he knew they were special, he passaged all the way round the old town, head held high, so proud to be serving his Master!

To end the night, Pepe drove the Master across the bridge into Triana, where the carriage halted in front of our flamenco tableau - Antonio claimed it was his favorite out of all Sevilla. If I close my eyes I can imagine the sounds of the horses stamping and snorting as they drew to a halt. I can see the garlands of flowers, the glint of diamonds in their forelocks. Evita always waited for the Master, she loved Antonio, we all did in different ways. When Ganador was sold to England she became hysterical 'He doesn't belong in England' she cried 'he's from pure Spanish lines. The English will never understand his pride. Ganador has spirit, he's not cold like the English' she was so distressed that Antonio bought her a pony, hoping it would take Ganador's place"

"Did the pony take Ganador's place?"

"No, how could he? Evita loved Ganador, she always helped with the horse, she held his reins and fed him sugar whilst the Master stepped down safely.

A crowd gathered round the horses the moment Antonio walked away… Ganador always drew a crowd. He was very clever. What you call a real character. He knew a lot of tricks; he could undo a man's tie with his lips! On one occasion he removed a pocket watch without the poor man noticing – and if anyone wore a hat he snatched it. He reminded me of a naughty child, a splendid beautiful child. Evita loved Ganador she never got over losing him. It means so much to have him here at her wedding"

"Did the horses stand outside all night" I tried to change the subject she looked so sad.

"When the carriage door clanged shut Evita gave the Master a rose and I took his arm and walked with him to his favorite table- as close to the artists as possible. After Ganador's show Pepe would take the carriage away to a quiet spot near the river. There are many wonderful sights and sounds by the Guadalquivir in the early hours" With a sigh she returned to the present... As she turned her skirt swirled around her ankles, her fan opened and closed with her simplest movement.

"Now I must help Evita" Once again she thanked me for bringing Ganador. Pepe bowed low, hand over heart; he pressed something into my hand and said "Muchas gracias Senora, hasta luego..." and again he broke into flamenco cante.

# 18. The Ceremony

During the afternoon there was a great deal of high spirits and at all times the need for song…It was always flamenco with a rhythmic accompaniment of clapping, finger snapping, and the shouting of encouragements to the singer.

The arranged music began at twilight, when a violinist played Irish folk songs, with an intensity I'd never heard before.

His special genius for musical expression brought tears to Mother's eyes, "Never have I heard a sound so beautiful" she sobbed "Reminds me of my family… I should never have left my homeland"

At dusk… two fires were lit on the sandy area close to the paddock. The fires had racks for meat, and large pots in which to simmer stew.

*

I remember that night so clearly, nightfall was the color of flashing gold… It's smells were of cooking, and smoke, which spiraled from the newly lit fires. The sound was of the tuning of Spanish guitars and murmuring voices.

Just before nightfall, I watched three older women lead a young girl into Mark's caravan. The third woman closed the door firmly behind them.

The girl's face was covered by a veil, and I felt the atmosphere change from high spirits to hushed anticipation. Everyone sat quietly now.... Geoff had returned from helping Mark with Ganador and Adams had taken his place by Mothers side. Several minutes later the same women walked out, faced the guests, and said the words.

"La Panuela esta bien"

On hearing these words the Romanies cheered and clapped, and I noticed a hanging basket of white roses had been placed over his doorway, and a golden ornamental dove stood at either side of Marks caravan. There was a feeling of secrecy about the ceremony... one I could not understand, and in a strange way it caused me to feel uneasy.

"The tall woman's the ajuntaora..." whispered Mother...

"Whatever's that?"

"She's the one who carries out the ritual" I started to feel edgy... surely there were no rituals, not now.

"The wedding can go ahead!" She sighed with relief.

A flamenco group had taken the place of the violinist; the performers sat in a semi circle - a guitarist played a Tarantas, the most beautiful of the flamenco cantes, with strange discords, exotic harmonies, and haunting melodies. As they played, the three women walked towards Mark carrying 'La Panuela'... a white cloth with three red rose petals embroidered as its centerpiece. The Romanies fell silent... the guitarist paused.

The three women now stood facing the young gypsy... they were singing "El Yeli"... "El Yeli."

Mark stared at the cloth, no-one spoke, no-one moved. Slowly, he nodded and then he bowed. Mark looked very proud, his black curls falling freely onto his shoulders... so very handsome dressed in his finery. A suit of black velvet, white silk shirt, crimson cumber band, a white rose pinned to the left lapel.

The atmosphere in the camp felt easier now, the tension had eased, people smiled and whispered.

I watched the three women walk from man to man until all had heard the strange words.

Only when the last man had been told did the guests clap and shout approval, and then there was a sudden hush...

Every eye now stared towards Marks caravan... slowly the door opened... And there in the doorway stood a young Romany girl, she was very young and beautiful.

She wore a white lace bridal dress, the bodice tightly fitted and cut low, her blue black curls falling down to her waist, wild and glossy as if abandoned. A shoulder length veil partly covered her face.

For a moment she stood in the open doorway, searching for Mark. She smiled when she found him, paused and looked towards him. Before stepping down, she held back her veil. The girl's skin was darker than his, her suave darkness contrasting sharply with the white of her dress.

At that moment, the silence gave way to cheering and clapping as she arrogantly walked towards him. Her gold dangling earings flashed as she walked – just visible through her white lace dress was an ankle chain.

In spite of her youth, she was provocative... meeting Marks stare with her own, head held high and full of pride.

The Romanies shouted "Bien casamiento!" and cheered. Mark looked stunned by her beauty – his lips trembled as she walked into his arms. He held her passionately, his black curls locking as one with hers. The guests clapped approvingly... the music dimmed, to a single haunting voice.

Pausing, he gazed at her beauty, and she stared him boldly in the eyes. And then he drew her to him and he kissed her. When he came out of his dream, heard the clapping – saw the staring faces he blushed and whispered something in her ear... and once more, his lips trembled.

The solo voice rested, a guitar played rapid cascades of notes, together with the tapping rhythm of a dancer – pulsating and intense. The music hushed to that of a whisper... no-one moved.

Mark held out his hand to the girl – woman, she laid her hand in his and still they stared...The atmosphere was emotional...and then he stood back. Carefully, he slid a gold bridal ring onto her finger.

At that moment the guests went wild, some of the men ripped up their shirts - they crowded round Mark singing El Yeli repeatedly as they danced in a circle surrounding him.

A guitarist swept his fingers across all six strings, weaving innate complexities of sound and rhythm. The Romanies urged him on with shouts of Olé, finger snapping the accentuated beats. For a second time the music reached a climax and a single voice blazed out over the guitar, the cante pierced the night air in a fervent cry to the heavens.

Each vow had now been sworn.... Every one of the customs fulfilled, exactly as the Romanies had wished, their ceremonies and traditions remaining unchanged for thousands of years.

Holding hands, Mark and Evita kissed. The flamenco artists stood and bowed to the bride. With one swift movement he lifted her into his arms, proudly parading his conquest for all to see... Evita was now owned by Mark, and would live in her husband's camp... for as long as they remained man and wife.

# 19. Ganador And The Dancer

'There's a feeling of excitement now, something special is about to happen…'

Exactly what, I didn't know, at that moment I spotted Ganador, he stood outside the gateway, striking the ground and calling out… he looked magical. His coat gleamed under the light; his mane and tail threaded with silk rosebuds, identical in design and color to the embroidery on La Panuela, the white cloth with the three red rose petals.

A small circle was cleared immediately to the front of the wagons… illuminated by a silver glow from the lanterns, and sparkling fairy lights. Numerous friends and relatives stood round… all holding packages.

"Solid gold jewelry" Mother pointed out "It's a Romany tradition" I looked on in total disbelief, never having seen such displays of wealth before. Mark rode in his usual Gypsy style… feet poked forward and body well back – without the hindrance of a saddle. The Romanies clapped in time to Ganador's trot… everyone wanted to touch him - calling out "el caballo blanco" His steps were high and hovering, almost floating…he was trotting the air, not the ground.

"He's enjoying showing off to the crowd" At that moment I recalled the quotation from a Spanish riding manual… whose words I knew so well:

'It should be plainly seen, that the Spanish horse enjoys carrying its rider, and being watched by spectators…'

155

"Perhaps he's fulfilling his destiny…." Geoff smiled.

"You could be right…"

The flamenco artists stood and clapped the spectacle of 'el caballo blanco' and then they began to play, creating rhythms, improvising melodies around Ganador's steps. The musicians and dancers built a passionate symmetry of sound and color. There was no set pulse from the music… instead it was completely free - its rhythm continually changing.

The flamenco, vows and ring were all essential to the rite, as was the presence of a white horse. Each ritual an important part of the ceremony… symbols of love virginity and reverence, traditions probably as old as the hills…

At that moment a dancer haughtily walked over to the stallion-she wore a tightly fitted blood red dress, so as to show the shape of her body, it left nothing to the imagination - neither did the color. Her blue - black hair hung loosely down to her waist, it was threaded with crimson roses… For a few moments she stood motionless… eyes half closed, absorbing the rhythm of horse and guitar. Then she launched into an explosion of movement and emotion, wild, passionate flamenco baile.

"Nothing like the flamenco put on for the tourists, is it Lass?"

"Oh no… this is real"

"Pure flamenco dance can only be seen at gypsy wedding celebrations"

"I didn't know that"

"Not many do… It's a Romany tradition"

It was easy to see why Mother felt emotional, for under the glow of lanterns the haughty Gypsy dancer and proud Spanish stallion were thrilling to behold.

The dancer moved her arms sensually up and down her body and through her hair, holding her hands high, she stamped rhythmically, in time with the stallions steps… And then she twirled to the left… and to my astonishment, so did Ganador. There was no rein contact, not that I could see – The stallion appeared to be dancing of his own free will. Striding backwards, she held out her shawl, and shouted Olé… and the horse advanced towards her in a high passage, he was snorting with pleasure. Without touching the garment, he reared high into the air; Mark was forced to hold Ganador's mane in order to stay on.

"He's enjoying this lark" Geoff looked cross, he must be thinking of all his ruined training time.

"I think he's amazing"

"Teaching a bad habit is never amazing..."

"Try to listen to the flamenco – there's nothing else important" All I could think of was the music, the cascades of notes, the evocative rhythms, I felt as if I was in a trance, hypnotized by its power.

The sound reminded me of when I lived in Sevilla with my parents... when I had been Mum's escort into the world of the back street Penas and gypsy bars. My Mother knew the places to visit to hear the best.... She was a flamenco aficionado.

During fiestas, she loved to stroll through the Triana district; to her favorite night spots... She said the left side of the Rio Guadalquivir was a very special place, another world.

So she didn't annoy Dad, she would book a room in a small hotel and take me along.

"Children are accepted... No one notices a child" Mum would say "But solitary females are strictly prohibited – in the Gypsy areas that is. This is our treat. Dad never feels happy with the Gitano's... he thinks we've come to Sevilla for the shopping!"

"I won't say a word he'd only worry if he knew"

Somehow our treats had carried on, I remembered last year in April, the month of the spring Fiesta. The flamenco bar we visited stood at the top of Calle Betis...At night, cars were prohibited - horse drawn carriages brought customers. I remembered the clatter of hooves on stone cobbles... the aristocratic men who stepped down... the gypsy girls who ran to meet them, always carrying a single red rose...

There were two guitarists playing now, their counter rhythms and melodies produced a dramatic effect. The sound was nothing less than orchestral. Unexpectedly, the music stopped, leaving the exposed rhythm of the martillo taps, mysterious and dark, a sound that always made me shiver. The dancer stepped backwards – so did Ganador, then she stamped forwards, the stallion watched her intently, copying her every movement. When the music returned horse and woman described pirouettes to the left and right, they were shoulder to shoulder. Ganador and the dancer moved as one. I must have appeared surprised, for I felt Mother place her hand on my arm. "It's not for us to question why Lass... Ganador's lineage is pure Spanish, the formulas in his blood" She was probably right. What else could it be?

"Is it a custom?"

"It's called, El Arte de Andalucia a Caballo...it's a centuries old tradition"

The mixture of music, lanterns, dancer and horse had caused me to feel dreamlike, I could have believed anything. The dancer bowed to the audience, and the horse dropped his head to the ground, it was uncanny. Everyone stood to applaud the show...and for the first time, the dancer smiled... then walked away.

At that moment Evita walked onto the paddock, she looked stunning, dressed in her bridal gown, with only one adjustment... her raw silk shoes had now changed, to the footwear of the flamenco dancer.

The Romanies cheered and clapped. Two of the men walked behind her carrying a wooden table top, which they lowered to the ground close to Ganador. Stepping on to the homemade platform, she immediately took up the proud stance of a dancer, head back, hips swaying, eyes closed. For a few moments, she listened carefully to the rhythms surrounding her... only her hands moved... and then she danced with her fingers. Holding up the palms of her hands, she opened each finger in rotation - just like a flower... she looked so beautiful. As the flamenco gathered speed, she held her skirts high. Her movements were free and fluid, torso swaying from left... to right. She stamped out lightning fast foot work, with a fiery passion.

Mark and Ganador described a circle around her, sometimes he trotted on the spot – moving high into the air, I had never seen such beauty. Several of the Romany women played castanets, or snapped their fingers in time to the rhythm, some even started to dance... the younger men threw off their shirts, and danced bare chested.

As suddenly as she started, Evita stopped, she stood motionless ... her arms curved around her head, in the opening position of the flower, and for a few moments, only her fingers moved. She stared into Marks eyes... everyone was aware of the chemistry flowing between them... it was raw, passionate, longing...

I watched Geoff carefully, I knew he felt uncomfortable, this wasn't his scene – he talked about engines, horses and farming – never women or sex.

"What's happening next?" he asked nervously.

"How do I know?"

"I'm just wondering" said Geoff regaining his composure "First there's a ritual, followed by a child bride and now it's looking like a prelude to an orgy. And I don't want to be around"

"Help Mark with Ganador then, he'll be riding him off anytime now" Mother had been so correct, when she said, "Anything can happen – It's Spanish" And I remembered Fernandos words when he told me of the Iberian combat horse, and his wish to please his master - 'at any cost.'

"He will die or he will dance, to please his master"

At the time, I didn't understand his every word was the truth. Fortunately the high spirits cooled down when Adams shoved his favorite arm chair into the Romany area. The wedding gifts continued piling up outside Evitas new home. The lid of the top box was opened wide, allowing everyone to see its contents, a one hundred piece hand painted dinner service in the finest china. The design was of horses exactly like Ganador, manes and tails threaded with rosebuds. On the plates were painted Romany travelling wagons, pulled by high stepping white horses.

When the guests had all admired this work of art, the men began pressing wads of twenty pound notes into Marks hands, some fell to the floor. I watched Pepe walking over to sit by Adams – he carried a wooden box on which to count out a large amount of money, more than I had ever seen before and enough to put a smile on Adams face. It must be a dowry? After the money was handed over a Romany youth stepped forwards and fastened a saddle bag around Ganador's neck, and the men carried on filling that up too.

This was the time when tables and chairs were prepared for the wedding feast. Adams and Mother sat at the top of the table together with Mariapi and Pepe, Evitas parents. Adams rose from his armchair, the same one that he positioned under the stars in summer...

"Tonight we thank the Lord for bringing Mark and Evita together" he shouted "May the blessing of the white horse bring you many children" He raised his glass, the guests cheered, Evita blushed. I watched Adams stagger to his chair. He was obviously the worse for drink.

As Evitas father began to speak, there was total silence, the kind of quiet only won by those who are respected. Pepe spoke in a rich Spanish, his accent unmistakably of Seville, one I knew so well, a guitarist translated his words into English.

"We give Evita to Mark, with joy and sadness in our hearts. I pray that he will always worship her beauties, and the gifts she brings to him. May your reward be many children" The sound of his voice rang with love and passion, it was a speaking voice I remembered so well, half sung, half spoken, the melody of the Gitano's of Seville.

The silence turned to partying, the tables were at last filled with food... there was lamb, fish, salad, fruit and hot sizzling meat stews. After everyone had eaten, Mariapi and the Ajuntaora carried a large wedding cake to the table. The top of the cake was decorated with three petals of a rose, identical to the embroidery on 'La Panuela'.

At ten, Geoff decided it was time to load Ganador and hit the road. Mark led Ganador from his stable to the loading area... the Romanies formed a passageway for him to walk through, first they clapped... and then everyone bowed.

"Bowing to a horse, whatever next..."

"I think it's time for us to leave" I whispered

"You're doing the right thing Lad" Mother said in a matter of fact way "Romany wedding ceremonies can last for up to three days"

At that moment, I heard Evitas voice, "Norma" she called "Gracias" and she handed me two neatly wrapped parcels, "Para tu, y Ganador" she looked so childlike. It was then I saw a locket of solid gold around her throat, attached to a ribbon of black velvet... the twinkling fairy lights must have shone on its inscription.

"Surely not" I felt astonished "This is Ganador's mark" for it was the stallions own brand. The one I'd examined so often, always wondering what it meant. The mark was the same seven peaked crown, and under it, a large S. It was exactly the same mark that Ganador had on his left flank. Evita touched the locket frequently, as if the image within was the object of love and respect. I knew she could not bring herself to let go – not yet. I reached out and touched the inscription, Evita looked at me blankly.

"Ganador wears this brand... How strange"

She glanced swiftly towards Mark... he stared into her eyes, and then nodded once. I'd seen this silent communication in the Gypsy districts of Seville, where a glance or an unseen movement said all the words necessary... removed the need for talking. An extra sense, almost primitive, of reading the others mind.

"Este es, la corona de Sevilla"

"Or to put it another way – it's the crown of Seville Lass" I saw Mark raise his index finger, the slight movement said all the words necessary, the conversation was at an end - and again he stared into her eyes.

"We have to go... it's been wonderful" Geoff wanted to be away, he'd a long drive ahead. Mark led Ganador up the ramp and into his stall, I could see the parting was upsetting him. And then the men closed the ramp with a bang, Ganador's shrill whinnies were at once muffled. So we embraced and said our goodbyes. Feeling exhausted and bewildered, I had a strange feeling that somewhere I'd seen Evita before.

*'Gypsy gold does not clink and glitter, it gleams in the sun and neighs in the night'*
*Irish*

# 20. Moonlight

Amidst sounds of champagne corks popping, and further tributes to the stallion, we prepared to drive away. As the engine spluttered into life, Adams pushed a fat looking package into Geoff's hand... in capital letters from corner to corner were the words FOR FAVORS RECEIVED ADAMS

Geoff tried to refuse the envelope... but it was too late he was already driving away.

Under the lights of the White Horse Inn, he slowly opened the package.

"Money!" he exclaimed "Crisp and new... All in twenties"

"How much is there?"

"£800!" he said smiling.

"Bet you never mention 'favors received' in the pub do you?"

"You're dead right... wouldn't make a good story"

"Well..." he said slowly.

"Well what?"

"The child bride, for one"

"Fourteen's average in the Romany world – or so I was told"

"Do exactly what they want though don't they, make their own rules? The powers that be probably gave up chasing travellers, centuries ago...."

"How can you chase anyone with no fixed home?"

"It's impossible, especially if they move around horse fairs – and use gold as a currency...Far more sensible to hound Jo public"

"What did you think about the wedding though?"

"Sexy" he said truthfully "The name of the game wasn't shied away from, that lot doesn't masquerade with singing hymns and spending money on honeymoons - Bless the marriage with a white horse, and bobs your uncle, all done and dusted"

"And you?"

"Ganador... and the Romanies" I said "He looked so content to be back with Mother and Mark... taught me a lesson...friends are far more important than surroundings"

"Not Pepe's invitation?"

"It would be nice to see a bit more of the Romany World... Especially as a guest"

"I suppose it's one way to see the district unmolested" Geoff had a point there, entering Gypsy areas without a male escort was frowned upon, dangerous even.

"When I saw the marking on Evitas locket, I thought I was dreaming"

"You are not going to believe what Adams told me – he said Pepe manages a famous Yeguada, which has the very same coat of arms as Ganador's brand!"

"Did he say anything else?"

"That the Yeguada is owned by one of the richest men in Spain. Like a palace it is, set in thousands of hectares and near to Seville. And listen to this! When Mariapi first laid eyes on the stallion at Appleby Fair... she thought he'd been stolen, and called the police!"

"I wonder if the interest of Police stopped him being sold."

"Adams told me Ganador was the talk of the Fair. He said nobody had ever seen such a magnificent creature... he also said that every night in the drinking houses of Appleby he told the story of Ganador..."

"Maybe he was telling fairy tales?"

"He probably was..."

"I don't suppose we will ever know the true story of Ganador"

*

Mist was rising in the valley as we entered the moorland road, and the earth steamed with spirals of blue tinted smoke... exactly like the camp fires had been only a few hours ago.

"Almost home" Geoff smiled and suddenly lost his tired look, he was back in his homeland "Just look at that view…. You can't beat the Yorkshire moors."

With a sense of gladness we turned down the track to the farm. I always had a feeling of perfect happiness when arriving home, like a warm glow, the kind you feel when the world is wonderful.

"It's going to be a lovely day" I said "Let's sit here and watch the sun rise… after unloading Ganador"

Shafts of gold lit up the sky from the east, shortly the sun would rise above the horizon with a golden haze falling upon the lower pasture.

Sue had prepared Ganador's box the night before, ready for him to walk into. Everything was just as it should be, thickly bedded with golden wheat straw; sweet smelling meadow hay packed tightly in its rack.

"What about giving Sue a special treat tonight? She deserves it doing all the work whilst we're away partying with Gypsies"

"Think she'd like a midnight ride over the moors?" asked Geoff "It's a full moon tonight, one of the brightest of them all"

"Sounds wonderful" and we walked back to the farm hand in hand.

That night, moonlight shone down on stone cobbles, a surge of silver sparkled on the rusty gate. The stable yard looked like a brightly lit stage in the middle of a dark valley.

For a few moments I stood there, breathing in the atmosphere of peace and remembering the magic of last year's midnight ride, September's harvest moon, the biggest moon of all. Memories of the night flooded back- eerie feelings when out on the moors with the enormous moon riding high, a sense of enchantment that I wanted to experience again.

There were three horses standing in the moonlight, saddled and waiting, Fred Donovan and Ganador.

"If we aim to set off about ten thirty" said Sue "I feel so excited!"

A full moon rode high in the heavens, painting the moorland

road with soft silver light, so different to its usual blackness.

Everything, even the long reeds had become works of art, their stems were radiant under the light, just like a fantasy of diamonds.

With Geoff in the lead, we rode up the alleyway by the side of the graveyard passing headstones edged in silvery light and crumbling stone walls etched as silhouettes against the glow of the moon.

Out on the moor's, isolated farms looked as castles mysterious, surreal. Their outlines burned in still white light and silver pathways led to unseen doors. Ganador pranced in passage throughout the ride, although on the whole he seemed calmer than usual.

"Might be the moonlight" said Geoff "Full moon's can alter behavior patterns"

"I think it's the Gypsies" said Sue.

"And I second that" I would never forget the Romany wedding; never forget the sounds of flamenco under moonlight, the colors and customs of that other race, the Gypsies.

Nothing mattered that night except the magic of riding Ganador under the light of the moon... and memories.

"I'm glad you brought us out" I whispered to Geoff.

"Thought you might enjoy it... Nothing like a full moon when seen from the moors"

\*

After the midnight ride I persuaded Geoff to prepare supper. Sue unsaddled Donovan and Fred whilst I stayed in the stable yard just wanting to be near Ganador. To place my cheek on his cheek, my hand on his magnificent neck and be aware of his energy. To look into his enormous black eyes- eyes that stared directly into mine, still and timeless.

And for a while I gazed at my creature from the Gods, content to be near him. I watched him standing there in the moonlight his figure a perfectly carved statue, the only missing item being his chariot.

After seven months on the Yorkshire moors Ganador's physical condition and beauty had improved beyond my wildest dreams. At long last the first step in repairing his shattered trust had successfully come to an end... and now there would be a quiet period before the start of part two- the most dangerous part.

*'With silver hooves and silver eyes*
*A silver horse came prancing by*
*I watched him cross a silver stream*
*Then disappear midst silver trees'*
*Moonlight by N Jimenez*

# Brief Index of Equestrian Movements and Terms.

Spanish Horse... Andalucian, Carthusian (Cartuhano) P.R.E. (Pure Raza Espanol)
Lusitano... Bred in Portugal. The Lusitano is now classed as a separate breed within Portugal.

Stud Farm.
Coudelaria... Horse breeding ranch - Portugal.
Yeguada... Horse breeding ranch - Spain.

Airs of the ground.
Piaffe... Piaffer. A rhythmical trot on the spot appearing to mark time. In the ideal Piaffe the forearm should be raised almost horizontal to the ground.
Passage... A highly collected trot that appears to hover. The forearm should appear horizontal to the ground and the hind legs step forwards under the body. In the soft passage the rider aims to capture the slow rhythm of passage but not the height.
Pirouette... Performed in canter or walk. The hindquarters mark the center of the circle, whilst the forelegs mark the circumference. The forelegs move around the hind legs and should cross.
Spanish Walk (Pas d'Espagne)... The horses forelegs are raised and extended forwards in each step of walk. Its knees should remain straight and the whole movement should appear graceful.
Spanish Trot (Trot d'Espagne)... The forelegs are raised and extended forwards, as in Spanish walk whilst the hind describe

energetic passage like steps. Demands power, ability and perfect balance.

Canter in Place (Ancient Canter)... The horse canters without moving forwards. Canter in place was first trained as a battle movement and used in the gineta skirmish, dual on horseback.

Canter to the rear... The horse canters in place and shows some movement backwards. This movement is rarely seen. Canter to the rear was needed by warriors in hand to hand mounted combat.

Levade... Prepared by steps in piaffe, the horse raises his forehand high with hind legs placed neatly under his body which show flexion in all three joints. The Levade began in combat, with less emphasis on correct flexion of hind legs and is still seen in gineta style riding.

Airs above the ground. (Leaps and jumps)

Capriole... The horse jumps high into the air. At the moment his body is horizontal to the ground he kicks out with both hind legs. It is believed this jump with its deadly kick back was used in battle to injure foot soldiers.

Courbette... A series of short jumps, off the hind legs without the forelegs touching the ground. The movement is performed from a levade or rear.

High school airs are divided into two categories: Airs from the ground and Airs above the ground. These airs demand great ability, strength and perfect athleticism.

Printed in Great Britain
by Amazon